'I would ve... why someon... ful as yourse...

'I'm not in the least defensive,' Kerith denied, which was a lie. 'And…'

'And you would prefer me not to think you beautiful,' Tris completed for her.

'No,' she agreed bluntly.

He gave a slow smile. 'I will try not to drag you into any more of our dramas,' he promised softly.

'If it concerns your son, I'd rather be dragged in than have him upset. I'm very fond of him. He's also been a very long time,' she added with concern when she realised that the young boy still hadn't come back.

Tris leaned back in his chair, and murmured, somewhat provocatively, 'He's leaving us alone.'

Emma Richmond was born during the war in north Kent when, she says, 'farms were the norm and motorways non-existent. My childhood was one of warmth and adventure. Amiable and disorganised, I'm married with three daughters, all of whom have fled the nest—probably out of exasperation! The dog stayed, reluctantly. I'm an avid reader, a compulsive writer and a besotted new granny. I love life and my world of dreams, and all I need to make things complete is a housekeeper—like, yesterday!'

Recent titles by the same author:

THE RELUCTANT TYCOON

MARRIAGE POTENTIAL

BY
EMMA RICHMOND

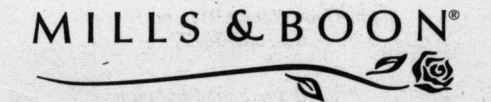

MILLS & BOON®

DID YOU PURCHASE THIS BOOK WITHOUT A COVER?

If you did, you should be aware it is **stolen property** as it was reported *unsold and destroyed* by a retailer. Neither the author nor the publisher has received any payment for this book.

All the characters in this book have no existence outside the imagination of the author, and have no relation whatsoever to anyone bearing the same name or names. They are not even distantly inspired by any individual known or unknown to the author, and all the incidents are pure invention.

All Rights Reserved including the right of reproduction in whole or in part in any form. This edition is published by arrangement with Harlequin Enterprises II B.V. The text of this publication or any part thereof may not be reproduced or transmitted in any form or by any means, electronic or mechanical, including photocopying, recording, storage in an information retrieval system, or otherwise, without the written permission of the publisher.

This book is sold subject to the condition that it shall not, by way of trade or otherwise, be lent, resold, hired out or otherwise circulated without the prior consent of the publisher in any form of binding or cover other than that in which it is published and without a similar condition including this condition being imposed on the subsequent purchaser.

MILLS & BOON and MILLS & BOON with the Rose Device are registered trademarks of the publisher.

*First published in Great Britain 2001
Harlequin Mills & Boon Limited,
Eton House, 18-24 Paradise Road, Richmond, Surrey TW9 1SR*

© Emma Richmond 2001

ISBN 0 263 82622 8

*Set in Times Roman 10½ on 12½ pt.
02-1001-36797*

*Printed and bound in Spain
by Litografía Rosés, S.A., Barcelona*

PROLOGUE

IRRITATED, anxious, *tired* Kerith continued her aimless perambulation round the waiting room. She had absolutely *no* idea why she was delivering her neighbour's nephew to his father in a French railway station! Why not his *house*? Why not a café?

Tall, elegant, she had an air of superiority that was totally unconscious, and a chic that women seemed to need to be born with. Her thick dark hair tumbled to her shoulders in disarray, framing features that were aquiline. She had grey-green eyes fringed with thick dark lashes and a wide mouth with a full lower lip as though pouting might come naturally. Her figure was full enough to be thought pleasing, slender enough to be fashionable. She was assured, confident—bossy—she would freely admit, and her way of wearing clothes was natural not artifice. She very rarely wore make-up, never preened in front of a mirror. In truth, she was usually so busy, she rarely had time to comb her hair properly. Her friends were dismayed by her lack of vanity and envious of her ability to be stylish by accident.

'He will come,' Michael reassured her with a smile.

'Of course he will,' she agreed. But what on earth

was she going to do if he *didn't*? They'd already been waiting an hour and a half. She could take him to the apartment she'd rented for her holiday, she supposed. Leave a message with the booking clerk.

'I expect he's been delayed. Traffic or something.'

'I'm supposed to be reassuring *you*,' she commented. Talk about role reversal. Halting, she stared at a poster. Her French wasn't very good, but she thought it warned about pickpockets. Not that there was any danger of that, they were the only people here. Unfortunately.

'Or, perhaps he came on time, and when we were late…'

'Only ten minutes,' she argued. Surely his father would have waited ten measly minutes. Although, if she hadn't booked herself into her apartment *first*, they wouldn't have *been* late. 'And why *here*?' she burst out. 'It seems a very strange place to meet.'

He shrugged.

'Doesn't your father usually pick you up from your aunt or your grandmother?'

'Yes, but he couldn't this time. We're going to spend tonight in the town and then drive back to our house tomorrow.'

'I see.' She *didn't*, but if those were the arrangements…

'Not been a very good day, has it?' he asked with a wryness not normally expected in a boy of eight.

Turning, she gave a small grunt of laughter. 'No,' she agreed. The ferry had been late, the roads congested, they'd had a puncture... And inaction drove her insane.

With a muffled sigh, she went to sit on the long bench seat beside him. They could have passed for mother and son. His tousled hair, although a lot shorter, was as thick and dark as her own.

'I wish...'

'What do you wish?' she asked gently.

'Oh, nothing,' he denied.

Wished his father wasn't always late? How many other times had he sat like this? Waiting for a father that never came? Which no doubt accounted for his insouciance. 'He'll probably be late,' her neighbour, Eva, had said with a dismaying lack of concern. 'He never does anything he's supposed to.' Hardly comforting when she had no way of contacting him.

She'd said he was a rat, a womaniser. But then, ex-sister-in-laws tended to be a bit bitter, didn't they? Sometimes. Mr Adventure. Charming—according to Eva—selfish, lightweight. Late. Glancing at her watch, she sighed again.

'We will wait, won't we?' he asked anxiously.

'Yes, of course we will.' But how long *for*?

There was the loud slam of a car door from outside and Michael leapt to his feet. 'That will be him!' he exclaimed confidently.

Before she could stop him, he rushed off and

Kerith got slowly to her feet. She heard his excited exclamation, 'Dad! Where have you *been*? What have you *done*?' There was laughter and the slow, unhurried voice of a man she did not know, had never met. There was no sound of apology that she could hear, no contrition—and she wanted to go out there and hit him. Did he have *no* idea what he'd put his son through?

'I knew you'd come!'

'Of course you did.' His voice was soft, pleasant, and Kerith's lip curled in dislike.

Snatching up Michael's case, she hurried out to join them, and then halted in surprise. She'd expected, dark, suave, sophisticated, but the man before her leaning awkwardly against the taxi he'd obviously arrived in, was none of those things. He was a tall, gangling sort of man, all arms and legs and a charming smile. He was also on crutches, his left leg plastered to above the knee. One trouser leg had been split to accommodate the cast, and he was wearing a revolting puce-coloured shirt. Don't get to like him, Eva had said. And she wouldn't. How could she like a man who treated his son so appallingly?

Michael was still talking, jigging around like a puppet with its strings crossed, his words all tumbling over each other in his excitement and relief, and she wanted to weep for the expression of hero worship on his young face.

'But what *happened*?' he demanded. 'How did you do it?'

As he smiled down at his son, Kerith had a few moments to study him unobserved. Crisp, light brown hair, somewhat disarrayed, regular features, and, yes, attractive, but not at all the sort of man she thought Eva's sister would have married. He didn't look as though he could find his way to the bathroom unaided, let alone navigate his way around the world, which he apparently had.

'And I wish I could say that I did it doing something exciting but, the sad truth is, I fell down the stairs.' His eyes crinkled in lazy good humour and Kerith's mouth tightened in disparagement. Michael deserved better than this.

Dumping the boy's belongings with an audible thud, she butted into their cosy tête-à-tête. 'A little bit of remorse for keeping us waiting might have been nice,' she snapped. 'A little bit of *concern*. And I have to go. Michael, don't forget your case.' Marching past them, she added crossly, 'And you shouldn't wear puce, it doesn't suit you.'

CHAPTER ONE

WILL you please stop *thinking* about him? She castigated herself as she emerged from the sea and trudged up the hot beach outside her apartment block. It was utterly ridiculous this preoccupation with a man she thoroughly disliked. Didn't know, she mentally corrected as she thumped down on the lounger and began to dry her hair. All right, didn't know. But Eva knew him, and Eva had said... It still didn't give you the right to be rude to him. It hadn't been his fault he was late. You can't *help* breaking your leg, but she didn't like men who traded on their charm. Her father had been like that. Expecting everyone to like them, fall in with their wishes. Expect to be forgiven for every misdemeanour, every excuse.

Kerith, she told herself impatiently, you aren't embarking on an affair with him. Don't have to live with him, see him, meet him. All you had to do was hand Michael over, be polite, and leave. So why the aggression? Liking him didn't even enter into it. No, but concern for Michael did, although he couldn't be *all* bad if his son adored him so, which he so obviously did. He was a nice boy. A caring, gentle soul, astute she would have said; so why, why, did he so adore a man who, according to his aunt, never remembered his birthdays or, when he did, gave him something totally impractical and not at all what his son had wanted. Never paid his school fees on time, never kept appointments... And hadn't she adored her own father who'd done exactly the same?

She sometimes thought that Eva hated him, blamed him for the death of her sister, but that couldn't be right; Ginny had died *after* they'd separated. She'd run into a tree whilst skiing and no one had ever implied that it had been *deliberate*.

'Kerith!'

Snapping upright with a start, she was astonished to see Michael hurrying over the sand towards her, his face a mask of anxiety. 'What's wrong?' she demanded.

'Oh, Kerith!' he exclaimed breathlessly, tearfully, 'Can you come? It's Dad.'

Thoroughly alarmed, imagining she knew not what—death, unconsciousness, heart failure—she scrambled to her feet, dragged her shorts and top on over her wet swimsuit, shoved her feet into her sandals, grabbed bag and towel and hurried after him towards the road.

'It's his leg,' he continued in fright. 'He's here.' He halted so suddenly that Kerith ran into his back.

'What? Where?' And then she saw him, much as she'd seen him the day before, leaning against a cab. Exasperated, *hot*, mouth tight, she glared at him.

'I'm sorry about this,' he apologised quietly.

'Sorry about *what*?'

He held her eyes for a moment, and then looked down. She followed his gaze—and saw that his toes were blue. 'Oh, my God,' she whispered. 'You need...'

'A change of plaster,' he said quickly. There was clear warning in his blue eyes as he looked up not to say anything further, worry his son. 'Can you look after him? I don't know how long I'll be.'

'No, it doesn't matter. Go,' she said urgently. 'I'm in apartment seventeen,' she added hastily as she pointed to the apartment block behind him.

He nodded, ruffled his son's hair and began the awkward manoeuvre to get into the cab.

'But I want to come with you!' Michael wailed. 'Oh, Dad, please. Kerith will come, won't you?' he pleaded.

'Yes, of course, but...'

'But you'll be much better to wait here,' his father completed gently.

'No! No. I won't leave you, I won't! I'm coming with you.'

'All right, all right,' he soothed. 'In you get.' He glanced at Kerith as his son scrambled into the rear seat and she nodded, climbed into the front beside the driver.

It was a silent drive to the hospital and when they

arrived he said quietly, 'I don't know how long I'll be.'

'It's all right. Go.'

He was seen straight away, whisked towards a cubicle and Kerith sat with Michael in the reception area.

'He will be all right, won't he?'

'Of course he will. The plaster is too tight, that's all.' She surreptitiously crossed her fingers. There had been strain in the blue eyes, lines of pain around his mouth.

'They'll take it off?'

'Yes,' she agreed. 'Put on a new one.'

'He was up all night,' he murmured. 'He thought I didn't know. He should have gone then, shouldn't he? If you leave things...'

Taking his hand, she stared into his young face, and reproved gently, 'Stop blaming yourself. He's all grown up.' She smiled. 'I'm sure he'll be fine.' And how fortunate she'd taken Michael with her when she'd booked into her apartment yesterday, otherwise he might not have been able to find her. The thought of her young friend in despair with no one to help him was almost too much to contemplate.

They sat there for over an hour before a nurse came to get them. She gave Kerith a rather quirky look, which Kerith quite understood. She must look a fright: hair uncombed after its rough towelling, damp patches showing through her shorts and top, sand between her toes...

'Mademoiselle Deaver? Michael?'

'*Oui?*' he whispered worriedly, and she smiled, said something Kerith didn't understand, but Michael nodded, whispered in English, 'She wants us to go with her.'

Kerith took his hand again and he held it so tightly he was in danger of cutting off her circulation. She didn't try to remove it.

His father was lying on a hospital trolley dressed in the ubiquitous gown that seemed to be the lot of patients everywhere, whatever country they happened to be in. It was also too short and came to just above his knees. Tanned knees. The plaster had been removed and she saw that his shin was puffy and discoloured. His toes were no longer blue.

He held out a reassuring hand to his son, then smiled at him. 'All right?' he asked gently.

Michael managed a jerky nod.

He glanced at Kerith and gave her a warm, rather teasing smile. 'I seem fated to appear before you in unsuitable clothing.'

'Yes.'

'I don't know how long this is going to take. A few hours at least. They want to rest the leg, make sure the circulation is OK before replastering.'

Michael stared at him almost fiercely. 'Really all right?'

'Yes,' he reassured his son as he continued to hold his hand. 'Really. Have I ever lied to you?'

Michael shook his head.

'We always promised, didn't we, to tell each other the truth?'

'Yes,' he whispered.

'Well, then, why don't you take Kerith to have some lunch? There's a café here somewhere.'

'No, we'll wait just in case something happens.'

'Nothing *will* happen. I've to stay here for at least two hours. You could go home, wait there.'

'No.'

'All right, but Kerith will be hungry, even if you aren't. You'll need money.'

'Mr Jensen...' Kerith began.

'Tris,' he corrected with a smile. 'Short for Tristram, but I expect you know that.'

'Yes,' she agreed shortly, 'Eva said, but I have some money.'

He shook his head at her. 'Michael will pay. There's some money in my wallet in the back pocket of my trousers.'

Michael obediently collected it, and when he had the money, gave his father a kiss. 'I love you.'

'I love you too. Go on, off you go. I'll see you later. Thank you,' he said to Kerith.

She shook her head and held out her hand for Michael to take. Time to go. His father looked as though he needed to be alone. He was probably in a great deal of pain, but she had to admire the way he'd reassured his son. Because she'd been there? Her father had always been at his most charming when other people were present.

They found the self-service restaurant without difficulty and, when Michael had paid for their sandwiches, soft drink and coffee, they found a seat before a large window.

'It looked a bit sore, didn't it?' Michael asked as he picked at his meal.

'Mmm, I expect it was. I've never broken anything so I wouldn't really know. Eat up,' she encouraged, 'otherwise you'll be hungry later.'

'Kerith?' he asked a few moments later.

'Mmm?'

Eyes on his plate, he blurted awkwardly, 'Don't you like him?'

'Like him?' she echoed to give herself time. 'I don't know him.'

'He likes you,' he insisted eagerly. Brown eyes fixed on her face, he added, 'He said you were pretty.'

Had he? She didn't want him to think her pretty.

'And he said you were probably a bit cross yesterday because you were tired. It was a long drive, and having to concentrate and, you know, being on the wrong side of the road and everything.'

'Yes.' Generous of his father not to disparage her after her rudeness, she supposed. 'We sometimes say things we don't mean...' she began. But she had meant them. Because his father hadn't, quite, been the stereotype she'd expected? Because he was far more attractive than she'd expected?

'It wasn't his fault he was late.'

'No.'

'And he threw the shirt away,' he added.

She gave a reluctant half laugh. 'Oh, Michael.'

He smiled at her. 'He put it in the bin.'

Yes, she could imagine him doing it. He would have given a wry smile, his eyes full of mischief. Just like her father when he'd been reprimanded for something. That charming lopsided smile, that sparkle of laughter in his eyes. They'd been blue, too— and she'd adored him, the way Michael adored his father. And then he'd left, when she was fifteen. He hadn't even said goodbye.

'Are you sad?'

She shook her head. 'No.' But she was. Sad for Michael, sad for herself because she was judging a man solely on the fact that he reminded her of her father—because Eva had said so. Not that Eva knew about her father, of course, but it was she who'd planted the idea in her head. And it might not be true.

'Kerith?'

'Mmm?' she murmured absently, and then smiled. 'Sorry. Wool-gathering. I expect your aunt will be in Greece by now,' she added in order to change the subject.

'Yes,' he agreed.

'You didn't want to go with her?'

He looked astonished. 'Why would I want to go with her?'

'Oh, I don't know,' she said lamely. 'Greece sounded pretty exciting, and I know she invited you. Don't you usually spend part of your holidays with her?'

He shrugged. 'Not really. I go to see her when I'm with Gran in the holidays, but I like being with Dad best. We do lots of things together. He's teaching me to sail.' His young face turning animated, he continued, 'We have this really terrific house near Parthenay. We're doing it up, and Claude, he's our builder, I'm teaching him English. There's a lake where we sail, and horses. I love it.'

'Good,' she said inadequately. Eva would like to see the boy more often, she'd told her that, but, apparently, she and Tris didn't get on, something to do with the way he'd treated her sister. She didn't know the details. Didn't want to know them. It was none of her business. And yet, whenever Eva *did* have him, more often than not, she left him with Kerith.

'Shall we go now?' he asked. 'He might need something.'

'OK,' she agreed gently. Quickly finishing her coffee, she got to her feet.

It was gone four when Tris finally swung himself out to join them. Replastered, a shorter plaster this time, just below the knee, and a teasing smile for his son.

'I have to come back tomorrow, just for a check-up, but then, *then*, we can go home.'

'It's all right here,' Michael said casually. 'I don't mind staying for a few days.'

'And that from a boy who's just been extolling the virtues of Parthenay?' Kerith teased.

He blushed, then asked his father, 'Have you phoned for a cab?'

'Yes, it shouldn't be long. Shall we wait outside?'

Now that it was possible to bend his leg at the knee, it was easier for Tristram to get into the car and at Michael's insistence, Kerith sat, reluctantly, beside Tris in the back.

'Can you come to the house?' Tris asked her after a few moments of silence as they drove back towards the small seaside resort where they were staying.

Horrified that he seemed to expect further contact, tense, she stared at him in alarm. 'Oh, no, I don't think so.'

'Seen it have you?' he asked with gentle humour.

'What?' she demanded in bewildered puzzlement.

He gave a little shake of his head. 'We'd like to take you out to dinner. To say thank you.'

'You don't need to thank me,' she denied quickly.

'Of course we do. Shall we say seven?'

Michael turned to look at her, his dark eyes imploring, and she began to wonder if he didn't want to be alone with his father in case something else went wrong with his leg.

'Just one more time,' Tris said too softly for his son to hear, and she knew he was laughing at her. 'Please?'

Without answering directly, she murmured, 'I'll need to go to my apartment first to change.'

'Shall we come to you?'

'No! No, I'll come to you.' That way, she could leave when she wanted to. 'If you could drop me behind the casino.'

He instructed the driver in fluent French and, when they halted, said to Kerith, 'About a hundred yards down on the left. It's the house with the blue door, just past the restaurant with the green awning.'

'I'll find it.' Giving Michael a weak smile, she climbed out and walked quickly away.

Dinner would be all right, she tried to reassure herself as she cut through the cafés and bars that decorated the sea front. As he had said, it would be the last time they'd meet. All she had to do was be pleasant, talk to him. That wasn't so hard, was it? Yes, it was, because she didn't *want* to see him any more. She didn't know about men. And that was so hard to admit, even to herself. She didn't know what to say when they flirted, paid her compliments, and so she became awkward and tongue-tied. Aggressive. She hated herself for it but she didn't know how to change. And, even worse, because of the way she looked, men assumed her behaviour was because she thought herself too good for them. Which was why she'd been so busily overreacting since she'd met Tris. Because he looked like a man who flirted, teased.

Two hours later, still reluctant, still defensive, aware, and embarrassed by the stir of admiration and envy she generated as she passed by, she walked along the tree-lined road to the house, and finally understood Tris's gentle humour. It looked as though it was hanging together by habit, or sheer force of will. Or maybe it was the trees that held it up; certainly there were enough of them. Plane-trees she thought, wide thick trunks that marched in unison down the long main road. Their branches met in places above her shutting out the light, but at least it made it cool.

Creepers almost obscured the windows, tiles were missing from the roof. The three steps down to the front door looked drunken and, if it rained heavily, she suspected that water would run into the hall.

With a little moue of distaste, she trod carefully down the uneven steps and tapped on the door.

Michael dragged it open almost immediately, as though he'd been waiting. He smiled at her. 'You look nice.'

'Thank you.' She smiled and suddenly wished, for his sake, that she'd taken more trouble with her appearance. She'd showered and changed, but only into beige trousers and a short-sleeved loose navy top. On anyone else they might have looked casual. On Kerith they looked elegant.

'Come in.'

Stepping not into a hall, as she'd expected, but into the main room, she heard Michael close the door behind her. 'Dad's just putting the rubbish out. I won't be long.'

With a last, happy smile, he disappeared up the narrow staircase. The staircase, presumably, which his father had fallen down.

She heard a door close somewhere ahead of her, and she stiffened, felt all her defences come into play. She didn't want to meet him again, not on a social level, not on any level. He confused and disturbed her. If he'd been as she'd expected him to be, it would have been so much easier.

Moments later Tris swung his way towards her. He was dressed in loose navy trousers that could accommodate his cast, and a blue shirt that matched his eyes.

He smiled at her. 'Come on in. Michael won't be long.'

Walking somewhat reluctantly into the room, she saw that the kitchen area had been divided off by a long counter, and even though walls had obviously been knocked down to make more room it was still hardly palatial. It was also dark. The front windows let in very little light due to the creeper that partially covered them and, at the rear, the glass doors that led into an overgrown garden were so covered in grime that it was like looking through water.

'Delightful, isn't it?' he asked easily. 'That will teach me to rent sight unseen.'

'Yes.' It also felt damp.

'It was all the agency had, and I thought,' he added wryly, 'that as it would only be for one night...'

'Yes. Why?' she asked bluntly.

'I'm sorry?' he queried in obvious confusion.

'Why stay here at all?'

'Oh, because it was convenient. I didn't know there'd been a change in arrangements. I was coming over to pick Michael up tomorrow but Eva said it had to be yesterday, and yesterday I had a meeting I couldn't cancel. I was expecting her to bring him herself.'

And he was angry, she thought. His face didn't show it, nor his manner, but he was angry about Eva not bringing him.

'He was quite safe with me,' she said stiffly.

'Yes, but if the accident had been more serious, if I hadn't been able to get to the meeting place, or get a message to you, then what?'

'Then I would have rung the hospitals, the police, and if that produced nothing I would have taken him to his home. And stayed with him,' she said positively. 'I'm not a fool.'

'No, but he's my responsibility, and where my son is concerned, I'm very protective. But thank you anyway—or are thanks not allowed from a man you dislike?' he probed softly.

'I don't dislike you,' she denied quickly. 'I don't know you.'

He grinned. 'And when did that stop anyone from disliking someone? No reason why you should like me, of course,' he continued easily. 'And we did get off to a bad start.'

'Yes. Mr Jensen...'

'Tris,' he corrected.

'Tris...'

'How *is* Eva?' he asked with that rather dry smile that so unnerved her.

'She's fine.' What else could she say? That she was dating an army of men who all looked unsuitable? And which was worrying Kerith to death. Eva was *not* discerning. 'She's in Greece.'

'Yes,' Michael said.'

He made her feel stupid, and wrong-footed, and that made her cross.

'We'll probably go home the day after morrow,' he added comfortingly, and she didn't *quite* like the small smile that lurked in his blue eyes. Amused him, did she?

Pulling herself together with an effort, she walked past him and went to peer through the grimy window. 'Michael said you're teaching him to sail.'

'Yes.'

'And that he's teaching your builder English.'

'Mmm.'

Turning, she gave him a look of mild derision. 'I hear the shirt's been binned.'

He gave a quirky smile.

'Pain in your leg gone?'

'Yes, thank God.' His smile turning self-deprecating, he added, 'Around three o'clock this morning I'd decided I was going to lose it. That it would definitely have to come off.'

'I'm very glad it didn't.'

'So am I.'

'It's going to curtail your—activities.'

'Mmm.' His eyes were definitely laughing at her, but she was darned if she was going to be the first one to look away.

'And if I'd dropped Michael off at your house,'

she continued determinedly, 'you wouldn't have broken it.'

'No,' he agreed softly.

'So why didn't Eva give me the address? We had to practically *pass* Parthenay to get *here*!'

'Perhaps she doesn't want us to get to know each other,' he proposed with even more amusement. 'And, had you come to the house...'

'*I* don't want us to get to know each other!' she interrupted. 'I don't *like* charming men!'

'You don't?' he asked in amusement. 'You prefer them broody and distant? Arrogant? *Very* uncomfortable I would have thought.'

Mouth tight, she glared at him. He looked back amiably. The silence stretched. She didn't want silence. Silence felt dangerous. 'You fly, don't you?' she demanded.

The devil in his eyes, he praised, 'Very good. Best to stick to safe subjects, and, yes, I do, although not so much now. It's a young man's game.'

She gave a withering smile. 'You're hardly *old*, Mr Jensen.'

'Tris,' he corrected again, 'and I'm thirty-seven.'

She nodded. Where on earth was Michael? She didn't *want* to talk to this man. She wanted to go away and not have to ever see him again.

'Thank you for your kindness to him,' he resumed blandly.

'Not difficult,' she murmured. 'He's a nice boy.'

'Yes, he is. And it was good of you to bring him out with you.'

It hadn't been good of her, she hadn't had much choice in the matter. When Eva had discovered that Kerith was coming to western France for her holiday, she'd promptly booked her own holiday to Greece and had asked Kerith if she'd mind returning Michael to his father. Not that she *had* minded, but it was a bit much that she hadn't told Tris. And if the grandmother hadn't been ill with flu, then Eva would never have had the ordering of it.

'You're an auctioneer, aren't you?' he said quietly.

'What? Yes.'

'Interesting, I imagine.'

She shrugged.

'And an expert on old jewellery and books.'

'Hardly an expert,' she dismissed, and then turned in relief as Michael thundered down to join them. He'd changed, she saw. Gone were the jeans and trainers, to be replaced by smart, long black trousers, highly polished shoes, and a white shirt. His unruly hair had been slicked back with either gel or water, and there was definitely the scent of aftershave wafting towards her.

Hiding her irritation with his father, hiding her smile, and certainly not unkind enough to comment, she murmured, 'I feel *very* underdressed.'

'No, no,' Michael assured her kindly, 'you look very nice. Doesn't she, Dad?'

'Mmm,' he agreed blandly.

She ignored him.

'Ready?' Michael asked.

'Yes.' More than ready. She just wished the whole evening were over.

Because of Tris's leg, they made rather slow progress along to the restaurant, and then elected to sit outside on the rear terrace—where everyone turned to stare at them.

'We look like a family,' Michael said happily. 'Everyone's looking.'

'Yes,' his father agreed, 'but then, I imagine that everywhere Kerith goes, people look, don't they?'

His son laughed. 'It's because she's so pretty.'

Extremely uncomfortable, because she *hated* being looked at, being the object of attention, she hastily took her seat. She had mentally geared herself for effort and then found, rather to her relief, that no effort was needed. She left the ordering of the meal and wine to Tris after she'd indicated her likes and dislikes, then listened as father and son teased each other. It was very obvious how much pleasure they took in each other's company. There was a bond there, a warmth, as though they knew each other very well, which, of course, they did. And Michael was so *concerned* for his father, which she supposed was natural. Every time Tris shifted his leg as though he didn't know where to put it to get comfortable, Michael would ask if it was all right, if there was anything he could do.

'I'm fine. Stop fussing.'

Michael gave a comical little grimace and turned to Kerith. 'Did you know Dad was an air ace?' he asked her.

'Yes, your aunt said something about it.' What she'd said was that he was always off playing with his aeroplanes and never there when her sister had needed him.

'Ferry pilot,' Tris put in laconically.

'Same thing. He's flown *everywhere*!'

'Must have been exciting. You collected aircraft from the manufacturer and delivered them to the customer?' Not that she cared, but the farce had to be played out, didn't it?

That amusement still in his eyes, he nodded.

'He liked the Piper Warrior the best,' Michael continued excitedly. 'It has an extra tank. All along the Eastern seaboard, Canada, Greenland. Thirty thousand feet over the icecap. Did you know that aircraft are ferried all over the world every week?'

'No,' she denied and forced herself to smile at him.

'It's what I'm going to do when I grow up. It's one of the last great adventures in aviation.'

Who had told him that? His father? Certainly it

seemed something he was repeating parrot-fashion, but he sounded so grown-up, bless him, so authoritative, although she doubted very much it was something his aunt or grandmother would want him to do.

'And what do you do now?' she asked his father as she finished her langoustines and pushed her plate to one side. Playboy? she wanted to ask, because that seemed the most appropriate and, if Michael hadn't been there, probably would have done.

'Architect.'

'Oh,' she murmured nonplussed. It seemed rather a staid occupation for someone who supposedly had adventure as his middle name.

'A lot of people are buying up old properties in France,' he explained lazily as though he knew exactly what she was thinking.

'Then, I expect you're very busy.'

'Yes.'

Michael finished his own meal, then tugged on his father's arm. They looked at each other, and Tris nodded.

'Would you excuse me?' Michael asked politely and then hurried off.

She assumed he'd gone to find the gents.

Cradling her wineglass, she watched Tris rather defiantly over the top of it.

He gave a lazy smile. 'Not long now,' he murmured.

She just stared at him. She couldn't think of *anything* to say.

'Michael said he sees you quite a lot when he's staying in England,' he murmured.

Slightly alarmed, wary, because she didn't want Eva later accusing her of telling tales, she looked down. 'Not a lot, no. Eva only has him to stay Friday nights whilst his grandmother plays bridge.'

'And Saturdays.'

'Well, yes, and Saturdays.' Which was when she usually saw him.

The amusement in his blue eyes deeper, he drawled, 'I'm not trying to trap you. I know very well that Eva has an active—social—life, and that he spends most of Saturday with you. I was merely grateful for your kindness.'

'Oh.'

Unable to comment, she continued to stare into her wine. She knew he was watching her, assumed he was still amused.

'And I would very much like to know why someone as stunningly beautiful as yourself is so defensive.'

She took a deep breath, and then looked up. 'I'm not in the least defensive,' she denied, which was a lie, 'and...'

'And you would prefer me not to think you beautiful,' he completed for her. 'In fact, you don't want me to think anything about you at all, do you?'

'No,' she agreed bluntly.

He gave a slow smile.

Refusing to look away, making herself continue eye contact, and not knowing what else to say, she blurted the first thing that came into her head. 'It was fortunate I was on the beach this morning, otherwise you might never have found me.'

'And fortunate that Michael knew where you were staying,' he drawled as his eyes continued to hold hers. 'I didn't want him to be there alone if...well, if things were going to be bad,' he explained. 'He's had enough in his young life to cope with.'

'Yes, the break up of a marriage is never easy for children, is it?' she asked tartly. 'You don't really know how much it affects them.'

'He was a *baby*, Kerith.'

'Even so. And then for her to die so tragically.'

'Reproof, Miss Deaver?'

'Don't be silly. Anyway, it's none of my business,' she added stiffly.

'No,' he agreed, 'but do I gather from your voice that your own parents were separated?'

'Yes.' Did the hurt still show? She guessed it must do. Certainly it had made her into what she was today.

He nodded, but thankfully didn't make any further comment on that subject, merely continued with his earlier explanation. 'It was a reasonable guess that you might be on the beach. It's usually most people's first port of call at the beginning of a holiday.'

She wasn't *most* people, and she didn't want to be thought...predictable.

'I will try not to drag you into any more of our dramas,' he promised softly.

'If it concerns Michael, I'd rather be dragged in than have him upset. I'm very fond of him. He's also a very long time,' she added with slight concern.

He leaned back in his chair, cradled his own wineglass, and murmured, somewhat provocatively, she thought, 'He's leaving us alone.'

CHAPTER TWO

'WHAT?' Snapping forward in her chair, she demanded, '*What?*'

'Leaving us alone,' he repeated. 'Don't encourage him, will you?'

'*Encourage* him? Are you mad?'

He laughed, sounding genuinely amused. 'I would have to be, wouldn't I?'

'Yes, you would,' she agreed fervently. 'You can't imagine I've been *promoting* this, this...'

'Intimacy? No. You don't have a current boyfriend, you see.'

'So? Michael surely can't think we'd have an *interest* in each other!'

'Hopes,' he said softly. 'He extols your virtues at every given opportunity.'

'How utterly boring for you.'

He grinned and she had to look away because it was a grin of pure mischief and conspiracy and very, very, appealing. Hardening her heart, she stared into her wineglass.

'He doesn't extol mine?' he asked interestedly.

'No,' she denied firmly. But he did. She'd thought it was because he was so proud of his father, wanting to talk about him when presumably he couldn't talk about him with his aunt or grandmother. Looking up, she found him still watching her. 'All right,' she agreed with a shrug, 'he does talk about you.'

'But it didn't occur to you that he was matchmaking?'

She shook her head, and then paused, because she'd had an inkling, hadn't she? At the hospital. 'He asked me if I didn't like you,' she murmured slowly. 'Seemed anxious.' And he'd said, hadn't he, that they seemed like a family. 'Oh, Lord!' she exclaimed.

'Not to worry,' he comforted in amusement. 'I'm sure he'll get over it.'

'It isn't *funny*!'

'No, but you weren't intending to laugh at him, were you? You're much too kind. Would you like a sweet? Coffee?'

'Just coffee, thank you,' she agreed absently.

Sipping her wine, she thought back over all those long conversations she and Michael had had. Despite what she'd said to Tris, Michael did come to her flat quite a lot when his aunt was looking after him. Not always because Eva was out. 'But why on earth does he want you to marry again?' she asked in surprise. 'I assume that is what this is about?'

'Mmm.'

'I thought he liked having you to himself. It's

always, "Me and Dad did this, or that. Me and Dad went here, there..."' Breaking off, she smiled at the waitress when she put her coffee before her, and then resumed, 'I always got the impression that he was quite happy with it being just you and him. Of course, he won't remember his mother.'

'No,' he agreed quietly.

How sad. 'Does he talk about her much?'

'Sometimes. I shan't marry again,' he stated.

As though she cared. Looking up, she said, 'You can't know that.'

'I can,' he argued.

'You might fall in love.'

'I might.'

Searching his face, a face she was becoming more and more familiar with, she pursed her lips. 'But you still won't marry.'

'No.'

Because of his ex-wife, she wondered? Because marriage had been such a bad experience? Because, despite the separation, he'd loved Ginny very much? Or was it because he knew he wasn't husband material? Catching movement from the corner of her eye, she turned her head and saw Michael marching towards them, his hands behind his back. He looked so comically smug that she had to smile.

He came to stand beside her, and then produced the package he'd been hiding behind his back. 'To say thank you,' he announced as he handed it over, and then he spoilt it all by adding worriedly, 'I hope you like it. It might not be…'

His father put a finger across his lips and said firmly, 'You know she will like it because you chose it specially. Never, ever, hint to a lady that she might not like something.' His eyes were alight with love and laughter as he stared into his son's brown eyes, and then he put his arm round his shoulders and gave him a little shake, a hug. 'Well done.'

Michael beamed and turned his attention back to Kerith.

Bemused and touched, she smiled at him. 'I don't know what to say.'

'Thank you,' Tris put in drily, and she gave a reluctant smile.

'I know, I know, whether it be praise or presents, ladies should always say thank you. Thank you,' she said to the boy. 'May I open it now?'

'Yes.' Michael looked as happy as though it was a present he'd been given himself.

Carefully untying the green ribbon, she parted the paper to reveal a box of handmade chocolates. 'Oh, how lovely!' she exclaimed softly. Looking up at him, she teased, 'How did you know I was a chocaholic?'

'Guessed,' Michael said promptly and she laughed again.

'Thank you. It's the nicest present I've ever had.'

Leaning forward, she kissed his cheek, and he blushed. 'Want one?'

'Can I?'

'Of course.'

A slight frown in her eyes as Michael pondered which one to take, she wondered if he'd gone on his own to get them. A bit dangerous she would have thought. He was only eight.

'The restaurant owner's wife went with him,' Tris said softly as though he knew very well what she had been thinking. 'We arranged it earlier.'

She flicked him a glance and then looked as quickly away. 'I didn't mean to imply otherwise.'

'Yes, you did.'

Yes, she had. As Michael returned to his seat, she chose a chocolate herself and offered the box to his father.

He shook his head.

Embarrassed, she fought to regain her composure. 'Well!' she exclaimed brightly. 'I've been thoroughly spoilt, haven't I? A delicious meal, a box of my favourite chocolates. A lovely start to my holiday.'

'Beautifully said,' Tris derided.

She deserved that. Not that it made it any easier to take.

He leaned back in his chair and watched her thoughtfully. 'Have you made any plans?'

Very conscious of his earlier words about his son,

she said quietly, 'Oh, I intend to go into La Rochelle, Rochefort, Royan maybe. I shall investigate markets, cognac, as this is the cognac region of France, and in between times I shall lay on the beach and be thoroughly lazy.'

'Won't you be lonely on your own?' Michael asked.

'Good Heavens, no! I like being on my own. No one to consult about what to do, no arguments. I can do exactly as I please. As you can,' she added with another smile. 'All that sailing to master, English lessons for the builder. Riding, swimming...' Picking up her nearly empty wineglass, she toasted father and son, although it was Michael she kept her eyes on. 'Thank you for a lovely meal, and I'll see you on your next visit. You can tell me all about the things you've been doing.'

Looking a little bit crestfallen, Michael said, 'We could stay here for a bit.'

'Nonsense. Why on earth would you want to do that?' Leaning across the table, she squeezed his hand. 'Think of all the things we'll have to talk about when we meet up again.' Turning her attention to his father, she forced another smile. 'I hope your leg mends well, and now I must go. It's been a busy day. No, don't get up,' she added hastily. 'Stay and finish your wine. Goodbye. Goodbye Michael.'

'Bye,' he echoed sadly.

He'd get over it. By tomorrow he would probably have forgotten all about her. So why did she feel such a heel? It was a well-known fact that children were manipulative. And she'd behaved like a moron. Tris was probably thanking his lucky stars that he wouldn't *have* to see her again.

Walking slowly, trying to savour the warm night air, she took the long way round to her apartment. There were plenty of people about and so she wasn't worried about being accosted. Under normal circumstances she guessed they would have walked her home, but the circumstances weren't normal and the sooner Michael got it into his head that she and his father weren't likely to become an item, the better.

And even if she'd found him attractive, which she hadn't, she told herself firmly, there would have been no room for romance. She had her life planned out. It had always been planned out. And now that everything was beginning to fall into place she had absolutely no intention of jeopardising it. She had the chance to join a more prestigious firm, more money, more responsibility. He lived in France, she lived in England. Anyway, never, ever, would she become involved with a man like Michael's father. Like her own father. No, she suddenly admitted, he wasn't like her father. Oh, he was charming, certainly, but he had more depth to him than her father had ever had. Her father's charm had all been surface. Beneath the façade had been petulance. She didn't think Tris was like that.

She could see her father, now, for what he was. Had been, she mentally corrected. Her mother had received a letter from a solicitor a few years ago to say that he had died. Nothing else, no information about how he had lived after he'd left them. Just a few lines to say he had died, which meant, of course, that he must have left his old address with his solicitor for just such an eventuality; which also meant, that he had thought of them from time to time. Or, thought of them once. Had he regretted leaving them? No way to know, but she was able, now, now that he was gone, with no hope of him ever coming back, to view him objectively, with an adult's perception, as her mother did, and probably always had. Knowing she was going to be hurt, knowing she'd been batting on the losing side, she'd still fallen for his charm. Had maybe told herself she would be the one to change him and, when she hadn't, had become bitter. Was still bitter, even after all this time. And her mother's bitterness had partially shaped her own life. Made her what she was. A fool. A driven fool because it had always been drummed into her that security was more important than romance.

Was it too late to change? Probably, and security *was* important, she knew that. The trouble was, the Tristram's of this world made people care about them, care *for* them—and she had no time for caring. Not at the moment.

No, Tristram was quite safe from her. As she was safe from him. He'd made that very clear. Especially after almost implying that he didn't look after his son properly. She shouldn't have implied it, because she *didn't* know him.

So stop thinking about him, she told herself impatiently. Stop thinking about blue eyes full of mischief, crisp hair and a winning smile. About long limbs and a tanned body.

Leaning her arms along the sea wall, she stared at the empty beach. It looked magical by moonlight and, yet, no lovers walked hand in hand in the surf. There was a great deal of busyness behind her, noise and laughter from holidaymakers just going out for a meal, or just coming back and, yet, here, she felt as though she were in a little island of calm. Lonely. How absurd, she castigated herself, she never felt lonely. Because she had trained herself not to.

She wondered if father and son still sat on the small terrace, wondered what they talked about.

She didn't know how long she stood there, quite a long time she thought, before walking on to her apartment. She avoided all eye contact with any young men she encountered, because she had learned in her twenty-eight years, that it was best to do so. One look, no matter how brief the contact, and men seemed to think she was giving them the come on. She wasn't. She didn't know how.

It was too hot to sleep properly, and so it seemed that she spent most of the night thinking about Michael, about Tris, and why Eva should dislike him so. Perhaps it was because he was a constant reminder of the sister she had loved and lost. A sister who would never see her son grow up. And it was even harder on the grandmother. People weren't expected to outlive their children. Eva had implied that Ginny had always been her mother's favourite and so Michael would be very precious to her. But not Tris.

Tired, unrested, she got up at seven and went to fling open the doors onto the balcony. It was going to be another hot day.

She didn't consciously look for Tris and his son as she spent a lazy day on the beach, but every time she heard a child's laugh, she turned to look. She was concerned for Tris's leg, for Michael, she tried to tell herself.

Feeling unsettled, she walked up to one of the cafés to have a coffee. Seated outside, the yellow raffia fringe of the umbrella above her wafting gently in the welcome breeze, she gave a violent start as Tris lowered himself beside her. She glared at him and he smiled back. A lazy smile, full of good humour.

'The leg's fine,' he taunted softly.

'Good.'

'I knew you were about to ask.'

She turned away, stared defiantly out to sea. 'Where's Michael?'

'Over there.' He pointed and she identified his son as he played with some other children on the beach.

'And so you're at a loose end.'

'No, I'm in need of a coffee. Would you like another?'

'No, thank you,' she said stiffly.

He summoned the waiter with easy skill, ordered his own coffee and idly picked up a paper napkin from the table in front of them. Within moments he had cleverly fashioned a rose, and handed it to her. 'One of my talents.'

'One of many,' she said without thinking. 'Don't you ever take anything seriously?'

'Michael,' he said without reprimand.

Yes, Michael. And his job perhaps. Architects weren't exactly known for their levity, were they?

She doubted he took his affairs seriously, and there had been a legion of those—or so Eva had said. She'd hinted that that had been the cause of the breakup of his marriage. Or one of them. Flying had been another, hadn't it? Had there been a girl in every port? Or airport, as the case may be.

Kerith believed it could be true. He looked the sort of man to have affairs. And why do you care Kerith? She didn't. Aware of the warmth that seemed to emanate from him, aware of his arm so close to her own, she panicked, because she didn't know how to deal with—feelings. 'I have to go,' she announced abruptly. Quickly finishing her coffee, she got to her feet. 'Goodbye.'

She dodged through the café, awkwardly manoeuvred herself between tables and chairs so that he wouldn't be able to watch her walk away and then had to double back because she needed to go to the supermarket to get something for her tea. Idiot, she scolded herself. Fool. Run away, why don't you? How much would it have hurt to stay and talk to him for five minutes? Hating herself, wishing she could be different, she pushed rather violently into the local shop.

And tomorrow, they would be gone.

The two weeks of her holiday went too fast, as holidays always did. She'd done all the things she'd intended to do, toured the markets, the shops in the big towns, even taken a boat trip to Iles d'Aix where Napoleon had been briefly imprisoned before being taken to St Helena and, all the time, during all her activities, a man with blue eyes stayed in her mind like an unwelcome ghost.

Tanned and fit, she returned to work—and mentally ticked off the days until Michael would be over for his visit to his aunt. Why, she wondered? So that she could find out about his father? How utterly absurd.

As it happened, she was away in Bristol checking out a crate of rare books when he returned and so she didn't see him. She didn't see Eva either, or not until the end of August. Eva knocked on her door on a Monday morning, just as Kerith was about to leave for work.

'Hi.' She grinned.

'Well, that's a fine greeting from someone who's been missing for the past six weeks. Where on earth have you been?'

'Greece, I told you.'

'For a fortnight!'

'Yes, well, I met this rather gorgeous man.'

'Eva!' she expostulated.

Unrepentant, she grinned. Shorter than Kerith, thinner, a few years older, her dark hair cut in a fashionable bob, she was as brown as a berry.

'But what about your *job*? They surely haven't kept it open all this time!'

'No. I gave it up. And now I'm going back.'

'To work?'

'To Greece. And there's no need to look like that,' she reproved. 'Don't be so *staid*! I shall be back on Friday to pick Michael up from my mother.

He's staying with her this week. So, what did you think of him?'

'Who?' she asked in bewilderment.'

'Tris, of course! I hear he broke his leg.'

'Yes,' she agreed cautiously.

'And Kerith came to the rescue!' she said somewhat derisively. 'Well,' she added impatiently, 'What did you think?'

'I don't think I thought anything,' she lied.

'Don't tell fibs. Tris is not the sort of man women feel *nothing* for. Attractive devil, isn't he? All twinkling eyes and rakish charm.'

'Not to me,' she denied stiffly. 'I don't like men like that.'

'Just as well,' she retorted. 'He'd run rings round you. Anyway, he goes more for the fluffy blonde,' she said tartly. 'They don't expect commitment. You, on the other hand, would expect a ring, wouldn't you?'

'Not with your ex-brother-in-law, no. And I have to go, I'm late.'

Eva grinned. 'OK. We'll talk when I get back from Greece. Be good.' With a little wave, she walked back towards her flat, and then halted. '*Really* didn't like him?' she turned back to ask.

'No.'

'Good. See you Friday.'

Except she didn't.

* * *

Expecting Eva when her doorbell rang late on Friday evening, Kerith was totally astonished to find Tris waiting there.

'Hello, Kerith,' he greeted quietly.

She just stared at him.

As he stared at her. 'I think I'd almost forgotten just how beautiful you were,' he murmured, and then gave a funny little shake, a rueful smile. 'I'm sorry about this.'

'Sorry about what?'

'I came to pick up Michael.'

'Michael?' She frowned. 'But Michael isn't here.'

'No, I know. He's with his grandmother. She thought you might have a key to Eva's apartment.'

'Eva?'

'Yes.' He gave a sudden sigh and ran one hand through his hair. 'I'm sorry, I seem to have lost the plot somewhere along the way. Eva's had an accident and I need to pick up some of her things. She's all right,' he added at her look of concern, 'a few broken ribs and concussion. She'll be fine, but Lena didn't have a key.'

'Lena?'

He gave a small smile. 'This is turning into a saga, isn't it? Michael's grandmother,' he explained, 'She said Eva sometimes leaves you her spare key when she's away.'

'Yes. No.' Shaking her head at her own lack of wit; and if he'd lost the plot, she thought, then she hadn't even seen the play. She took a deep breath and tried again. 'Yes, she sometimes leaves me a key,' she said firmly, 'but not this time. Is she really all right?'

'Yes.'

'So, what will you do now?'

'Phone a locksmith?' His eyes crinkled with amusement and she almost smiled back. Almost. 'May I come in for a moment?'

'Oh, yes, yes of course. I'm sorry. You took me by surprise.' Holding the door wider, she let him in and then found herself squashed into a space barely big enough for one, let alone two. Hurriedly shutting the front door, she squeezed past him and led the way into the lounge. 'What sort of accident was it?'

'Jet-ski,' he murmured as he put the grip he was carrying at his feet. A grey sweater was folded tidily on top, a grey sweater that would match the grey polo shirt he was wearing. He no longer wore the plaster on his leg.

'Have you just arrived?' she asked stupidly, and it *was* stupid, because he wouldn't be carrying his grip if he hadn't.

'Yes.'

Confused and angry by her behaviour, she said abruptly, 'I'll make you a coffee.' She walked quickly into the kitchen and then just halted, took several deep breaths. She'd forgotten how tall he was, how gangling... No, she hadn't, she thought disgustedly. She'd remembered every blessed thing about him.

Taking out the cafetière, she began spooning coffee into it—and then remembered to put the kettle on. She heard him come out behind her and she stiffened. 'Have you eaten?'

'No.'

Turning, she looked at him. His hair was longer, his face browner. He also looked tired and ruffled. Endearing. Shut up Kerith.

'Would anyone else have one?' he asked as he returned her appraisal.

'One?'

'Key,' he explained quietly.

'Oh. No.' Feeling stupid, she turned back to finish making the coffee. 'How did you find out about the accident?' she asked curiously.

'Eva's—friend—rang me from Greece.'

The fabulous man she had met Kerith supposed. And did Eva usually ring him when she was in trouble? A bit odd, she would have thought; Eva always made out that Tris was arch-enemy number one. 'Why didn't he ring Eva's mother?' she asked curiously.

'I don't know.'

No, why would he? 'How do you take your coffee?'

'Black, thank you.'

'I could make you a sandwich, or something...' she offered as she pushed down the plunger on the coffee.

'No, that's all right, I'll get something to eat later.'

'It is later.' Pouring the coffee, she handed it to him. 'I can make you, oh, I don't know, omelette? Egg? Bacon? Beans on toast?' Why? Why was she asking him this? She didn't want him here.'

'Whatever's easiest.'

'Tristram! Just give me a clue, will you?'

'Omelette.'

'Thank you.'

'With beans?'

'With beans,' she agreed.

Very aware of him leaning against the worktop sipping his coffee and watching her as she cooked, she asked stiffly, 'Does Michael know about his aunt?'

'Yes, I rang as soon as I knew.'

'He'll be upset.'

'Yes,' he agreed noncommittally.

She sent him a brief glance and murmured without thinking, 'Doesn't have much luck with his relatives, does he? Broken leg, broken ribs, what is it with your family?' And then remembered, too late, the accident to his wife that had robbed her of her life. Horrified, she whirled to face him. 'I'm sorry,' she apologised quickly. 'That was insensitive.'

'But understandable. Don't fret about it, Kerith.'

'No.' But she did, she really must learn to think before she spoke. She couldn't even put it down to his unsettling presence. She often spoke without thinking. Because she was impatient. Because she liked an ordered life. 'Will you go out to see her?' she asked as she dished up his omelette and beans.

'To take out the things she wants from her flat, yes.'

'Her mother will be worried.'

'Stop fishing Kerith,' he reproved gently as he took the plate from her.

'I wasn't!' she denied.

'Weren't you?'

'No!' But maybe she had been. Maybe.

'Implements?'

'What? Oh, sorry.' Taking a knife and fork from the drawer she indicated he walk through to the lounge. Following him, she drew up a small table for him to use, then returned to the kitchen for salt and pepper and bread and butter.

Had she annoyed him? she wondered. 'I'm sorry,' she apologised again as she handed him the bread and butter. 'It's really none of my business.'

'No,' he agreed gently.

'Is there anything I can do?'

He shook his head. 'Not unless you know of a

good locksmith who's prepared to come out in the evenings.'

'No,' she said. Seating herself in the armchair opposite, she watched him eat. Each movement tautened the material of his shirt across his broad back, flexed the muscles in his forearm. Daft woman, she scolded herself, he's just a man.

But he wasn't. He was Michael's father, Eva's ex-brother-in-law. A rat. He didn't look like a rat.

'Do you know of any bed and breakfasts near here? The hotel I usually book into was full. Some sort of convention.'

She jumped. 'No,' she denied hastily. Glancing at the clock, she saw that it was nearly midnight. Much too late to go looking for somewhere to stay. 'You can use my spare room,' she offered. She hadn't meant to say that. She didn't want him here. He unsettled her and she didn't like to be unsettled.

He looked up, his blue eyes holding hers. 'Sure?'

'Well, of course I'm sure!' she said impatiently. 'Why wouldn't I be?'

'My reputation?' he asked softly.

So he did know Eva talked about him. Well, why wouldn't he? Eva wasn't the sort of woman to say things behind his back. She would have said them to his face. Which was why, in France, he'd known what she was thinking when Michael had gone to get her chocolates, she supposed. He would know, or suspect, that Eva had denigrated his care of his son to her. 'I don't imagine you're likely to force yourself on me. Are you?'

'No.' He put his knife and fork tidily on his plate and leaned back. 'Thank you,' he said quietly. 'I'd be very grateful.' He gave a small smile. 'I don't *quite* fancy tramping the streets at this time of night.'

'No. More coffee?' Springing to her feet without waiting for him to answer, she picked up his plate and carried it into the kitchen.

'You said you have to pick Michael up,' she called back as she put the kettle on to boil.

'Tomorrow morning.'

She jumped at the sound of his voice so close behind her. Why couldn't the wretched man stay in one place?

'And could you not stay at—Lena's, was it?'

'No.'

No. Because Lena didn't like him? Didn't have room? 'And your leg? Is it all right now? I'm sorry, I forgot to ask.'

'It's fine.'

In France, he had smiled a lot. He didn't seem to be smiling now. Perhaps he was worried about Eva. Perhaps he was even *fond* of her.

'How did you get here from the airport?' she asked to fill the silence.

'Cab.'

'So you don't have a car with you?'

'No. Why don't you go to bed?' he asked softly. 'You don't have to entertain me.'

'No,' she agreed. But she felt that she did. She waved her hand vaguely towards the coffee makings and said quietly, 'I'll go and make up your bed.'

It didn't take long and, when she'd finished, she said awkwardly, 'Help yourself to anything you need. Shower, more coffee, whatever. Goodnight Tris.'

'Goodnight, and thank you.'

She gave him a lame smile and left him to his own devices. She used the bathroom first, then went thankfully into her room.

She could hear him moving around as she got ready for bed, nothing loud or intrusive, but it still kept her on edge, unable to relax.

She heard the shower running and remembered she hadn't put out clean towels for him. She started to get out of bed to rectify matters, and then subsided. He probably had a towel of his own. Or something.

She'd behaved like an idiot, she thought disgustedly. Tongue-tied, immature. As she always was. With men. Perhaps she could practise on him. Learn how to flirt, how to be comfortable with the opposite sex. Yeah, right Kerith, brilliant idea!

Tomorrow would be better, she assured herself. Now that she knew he was here, tomorrow would be better.

She heard the bathroom door open and the click the switch made as it was turned off. Heard his soft footsteps returning to the lounge, and then silence. She imagined him going into the spare room, climbing into bed. Was he thinking about her? Laughing at her behaviour?

No! Don't be a fool! Why on earth would he be thinking about her? He didn't like her. Why should he? If he'd liked her, trusted her, he wouldn't have been so cautious with his answers, would he? Cautious of your nosiness, you mean, she scolded herself. Yes, her nosiness—and she didn't want him to be as Eva said he was. Didn't think he was.

Maybe it was that hint of laughter that always seemed to be in his eyes... Or maybe it was the easy confidence he displayed. And maybe it wasn't any of those things.

The quiet click of the door woke her, and she snapped open her eyes in shock, stared almost blankly at Tris as he stood in the doorway holding a cup in his hand. He looked abnormally serious and she felt vulnerable. Barely awake, she blinked like a little owl, and he gave a small smile.

'Good morning. I brought you some tea.'

She mumbled something inarticulate and his smile widened.

'Not very good in the mornings, Kerith?' he teased.

She grunted.

'I, of course, leap out of bed with amazing vigour.' He carefully put her tea on the bedside table and went out. He closed the door softly behind him.

Fool.

He probably didn't even like her. Not surprising after the way she'd treated him in France. And no one leapt out of bed with amazing vigour! Did they? She felt a smile start in her eyes, and hastily banished it. Don't get to like him, Eva had said. Well, she wouldn't. Dragging herself up in the bed, she reached for her tea.

His appearance the night before had thrown her momentarily off balance, that was all it was, and she should get up, find him a locksmith, and then he would go. He would take Michael, and maybe Lena, out to see Eva and then they would return to France. End of. Finis. Schools went back next week—at least, they did in England; she didn't know if it was the same in France.

Getting up, she found her dressing gown and then padded softly into the bathroom to have her shower. She locked the door. Something she had never, ever, had occasion to do before.

She would be cool, in control, pleasant, she promised herself but, when she finally walked into the lounge, all her careful promises were thrown into disarray. He had one foot up on one of her dining chairs which now stood in the middle of the room and, as she watched, he slowly levered himself up onto it, and then down again. He had to keep his neck bent to avoid hitting his head on the ceiling.

'What on *earth* are you doing?'

He visibly jumped, lowered his foot, and turned to face her. He then burst out laughing. 'Caught in the act,' he said choking. 'I didn't hear you get up.'

'But what are you *doing*?'

His face still creased with amusement, he slowly replaced the chair. 'My exercises.'

'Well, please don't let me stop you,' she said in a faint voice.

'No, no, I'd more or less finished.' Laughter still shaking his long frame, he rested his hands on the chair back, gave her a sideways glance. 'How to impress a beautiful woman in one easy step.'

She just looked at him and his lips twitched again. 'It's to strengthen my shin bone,' he finally explained. 'The hospital devised them. I'm supposed to do them every morning.'

'Right,' she agreed. 'I'll go and start the breakfast. Egg and bacon?'

'Please.'

She could still hear him chuckling when she walked into the kitchen, and was then aware of him coming to lean in the doorway behind her.

'Did you sleep all right?' she managed casually.

'Mmm. It *is* all right to laugh,' he informed her.

'I wouldn't dream of it. It took me by surprise,

that was all.' Eyes creased in amusement, she bent to take eggs and bacon from the fridge. 'Toast or bread?'

'Toast, please. I used your local directory to find a locksmith. He should be here in about an hour. Can I do anything to help?'

'You can lay up the breakfast bar if you like.'

He did it quietly, as he seemed to do everything quietly. Including his ridiculous exercises, and she felt the smile come back into her eyes.

Indicating for him to take his place, she put his breakfast before him, made the mistake of looking at him, at the wry humour in his blue eyes, and her face split in a wide grin. His expression changed, became almost startled, and she felt awkward again, tense, because something had happened between them. Something different.

'Sorry,' she mumbled distractedly as she hastily dragged her eyes away, 'but you did look rather ridiculous.'

'I know,' he agreed, and his voice too, was changed. 'My ceilings at home are a bit higher than yours.'

'Michael said the house is big,' she continued desperately.

'Yes, too big for two people really, but we like it. The garden still looks like a building site, but we'll get there.'

'Must be very satisfying to get it how you really want it.'

'It is.'

They didn't look at each other again, and it seemed as though they both fought to make their conversation normal. But it wasn't normal, and it felt dangerous.

The doorbell rang and they both started.

'That will be the locksmith. No, don't get up,' he said quickly, almost in relief. 'Finish your breakfast. I'll see you later I expect. Thank you for letting me stay, and for the meals.'

'You're welcome.' And he was. Foolish as it might be. He was.

He didn't come back, and so she assumed that it had indeed been the locksmith. And when she walked into the lounge a few minutes later, and then into the spare bedroom, it was to find his grip gone. The bed had been made. No sign at all that he had ever been there.

She would no doubt see him later. Probably. But best not. Really.

CHAPTER THREE

How would he pick Michael up, she wondered as she stripped the beds? Hire a car? Get a cab? Walk? The grandmother didn't live that far away. She could have offered to drive him. No, she mustn't offer anything at all. She must stay away from him.

They were probably going to Greece straight away and then they would return to France. And she wouldn't see him again.

She finished clearing up, did her usual Saturday morning chores, and then went out to walk round the shops. People always seemed to find it astonishing that she lived in Streatham. She didn't know why. She rather liked it. She found the people friendly, the shops adequate for her needs and, although the properties weren't *cheap* exactly, they weren't as expensive as some other parts of London.

She had her lunch out, and when she returned it was to find an enormous bouquet of flowers lying by her front door. Picking them up, she extracted the card, and gave a silly smile at the picture of a crane depicted on it. It was standing on one leg. Just as Tris had been. The message said simply, 'Thank you. T.'

Had he found the card easily? Or had he searched

for it? Gone to enormous trouble to find one just right? He found it easily, Kerith, she told herself impatiently. Why on earth would he go to enormous trouble? She was no one. A neighbour of his sister-in-law. That was all. *All* she told herself firmly.

She put the flowers in water, took a deep breath, and then walked determinedly across to the other flat to see if Tris was there in order to thank him— And with superb timing, Eva's door opened and Michael emerged.

He was talking, obviously to his father inside, looking back over his shoulder, laughing. And she wondered, suddenly, quite out of the blue, what it would be like to have a son of her own. Someone who would laugh like that, adore her as Michael adored his father. The way she had adored her own father.

She hadn't given up on marriage, hoped that one day she would meet someone who would see through her shield to the person she was inside but, at the moment, her career came first. She wanted to get really established as a top auctioneer. There was plenty of time, she was only twenty-eight.

'Hey, Kerith!' Michael exclaimed happily. 'I was just coming to see you.'

'Were you? That's nice.' She smiled. 'I came to thank your father for the flowers.'

'Oh, that's OK,' he said airily, 'he likes sending people flowers.'

'Michael,' a quiet voice warned from inside the flat, and the boy grinned.

'I was coming to ask you if you knew of a DIY shop near here,' Michael continued. 'We need to mend a socket.'

'We?' Tris asked softly as he strolled out behind his son, and Kerith stiffened slightly, glanced at him, and then away.

'I can help!' Michael insisted.

'Mmm,' he agreed drily. 'Hello, Kerith.'

'Hello,' she mumbled inadequately. 'Do you need it now?'

He looked startled for a moment and then, as though he were going to say something and as quickly changed his mind, he asked carefully, 'Do I need what now?' He sounded different. As she was different.

'The DIY shop.' This was silly. She hadn't been this aware before they'd had breakfast.

'Oh, yes, the socket's dangerous.'

She nodded. 'There's one on the roundabout.' Confused and breathless, she added quickly, 'I'll go and get my car keys.' Turning, she began hurrying back to her flat.

'Kerith! No!' he called. 'I wasn't asking you to take us! We can get the bus, or something.'

Yes, Kerith, let them get the bus. She didn't want them to get the bus. Pretending she hadn't heard, she walked into her flat and closed the door.

It was no big deal. Anyone would have offered to drive them.

All right, she told herself defiantly, she liked him. *Wanted* to drive him. That wasn't a crime was it? It wasn't going to go any further. It couldn't. He lived in France, she lived in England. She had a career she loved. He had his own career. And just because he'd bought her flowers didn't mean he was attracted. Just because he'd sounded *constrained* didn't mean he was attracted. It just meant—he didn't want to ask her any more favours.

She deliberately didn't comb her hair, nor put on any lipstick, merely collected her car and flat keys and went to wait for them in the hall.

She heard them come out and she forced herself to look at him. He was just a man, she told herself forcefully. A nice man, but that was all. *All* she told herself.

He gave her a lopsided smile—and her resolution weakened. Turning away, she said abruptly, 'Thank you for the flowers.'

'You're welcome.'

She wanted to smile at him, be relaxed, but she couldn't, and so she led the way down the stairs.

'I was quite determined not to trade on your good nature any more,' he said softly as they descended.

'I don't have a good nature,' she argued. 'I have an *interfering* nature.'

He didn't say a word, and she wished, wished,

she could have given a flippant answer, could behave like other girls behaved, but she couldn't.

'Aren't you coming in with us?' he asked when they'd parked in the large car park.

'Whatever for?' she demanded in astonishment.

'We might need some help,' he said blandly. 'It's a long time since I lived in England. I'm not sure I know what fuse wire to get.'

'They do have *staff*!'

He waited, his eyes alight with—well, something, anyway. With a little tut, a pretend tut, she climbed out and locked the door. She wanted to be with him. She did—want—to be with him.

Leading the way into the enormous cavern of a store, she stared round her, then headed in the direction of the electrical section. She assumed they were following her. They weren't.

Turning back, she found they'd been distracted by the drill section. Were men totally incapable of buying just the things they needed?

'Hey, Dad, look at this!' Michael exclaimed and he was off. To look at a shredder? And then they discovered something that supposedly stripped wallpaper off without effort. And she wanted to be with them, laugh with them, hold Tris's arm, lean her head against him, put her other hand on Michael's shoulder.

Fool, she scolded herself. Fool of a girl. They didn't need her, and these feelings were getting way,

way, out of control. Deliberately turning her back on them, she went to get the things they might need. A set of screwdrivers for one thing, because she doubted Eva had anything suitable, fuse wire, fuses and a new socket. She returned to the shredder display, and found them gone.

She eventually found them playing with a working model of a system advertised to revolutionise anyone's abode. Dimmer switches, gadgets that turned on the television and hi-fi system, drew curtains... They looked happy and relaxed together. Laughing. In need of no one but themselves.

She gave an impatient little shake of her head. 'Eva doesn't *need* dimmer switches,' she informed them as she dumped their required items in Tris's hands.

He looked at her, smiled, glanced down at what she had given him, and reproved, 'You've forgotten the tape.'

'*What* tape?'

'Um, black stuff. I don't know what it's called.'

Neither did she. 'I'll meet you at the checkout... In two minutes!'

He laughed—and kissed her on the nose.

Astonished, she just stared at him. And then blushed. Furious with herself, she marched away and heard his soft laughter behind her. 'Come along, Michael,' he said blithely, 'we don't have time to play.'

'It wasn't *me*!' he protested. 'You were the one who...'

Don't get involved with him, Eva had said. And she wouldn't. She *wouldn't*. Leaning against some shelving for a moment, she closed her eyes. This was ridiculous. All he'd done was kiss her on the nose. She didn't even *know* him.

'Are you all right?'

Snapping open her eyes, she stared at a young staff member. 'What? Oh, yes, sorry, I was looking for the tape.'

If he thought it strange she was looking with her eyes shut he kindly didn't mention it. 'What tape would that be?'

'I don't know. Black, for light switches, sockets, that sort of thing.'

'Insulating.' He nodded, then smiled at her. 'This way.'

He walked backwards, his gaze fixed on her beautiful face and, because he was so young, and obviously no threat, she giggled.

He gave a theatrical sigh—and came to an awkward and abrupt halt as he walked into someone. Tris.

The young man turned, startled, opened his mouth to apologise, and Tris laughed, 'You'd do better to look where you're going.'

'I know.' He grinned. 'But have you ever seen anyone so beautiful?'

'Oh, she knows she's beautiful,' Tris murmured, his eyes alight with devilment. 'Don't you, Kerith? I found the tape by the way.'

'Well, really!'

'You didn't want me to find it?'

'Of course I wanted you to find it, but that wasn't what I meant, as you very well know!'

'Of course I know, the same as I know that you know you're beautiful. You aren't a fool. Are you?'

Yes, she wanted to say, I am a fool. I wasn't, but now I am.

'He would have done better to have told you that you look eminently kissable,' Tris added. 'Which you do.'

He walked towards the checkout where Michael was waiting and she followed numbly. Eminently kissable? Is that what he thought? There was the oddest little feeling in her stomach which she hastily dismissed, tried to forget. She hadn't thought about kissing him. She really hadn't. Until now. And, ever since their exchange at Eva's door, she kept getting the feeling that he was acting. Why? Because he, too, was pretending not to be attracted?

Don't be a fool Kerith. A man like Tris had no need to act. A man like that *knew* how to behave if he was attracted; it was only idiots like herself who didn't.

She didn't join in their chatter on the way home, she thought about kissing instead and, because she was preoccupied, she followed them into Eva's flat without thought.

He knelt to mend the socket and she stared at him. He had a good profile: strong, determined. His hair just touched the collar of his shirt. It looked silky, clean, in need of touching.

He glanced at her, and she looked quickly away, stared deliberately at the picture of his dead ex-wife that stood on the television. He's not for you, Kerith. No. With a determined little breath, she returned her attention to him, watched his nimble fingers as he stripped wires. She glanced at his son, who was hovering less than helpfully, his face a study in concentration, as though he were remembering every move, everything he needed to know in order to rewire and replace a blown socket.

She opened her mouth to tell him not to try it himself, and then closed it. It wasn't for her to tell Tris's son anything.

Within half an hour it was all done.

'Not entirely useless,' Tris taunted her softly from very close quarters.

She took a hasty step back. 'I never said you were.'

'Implied.'

Yes, implied, and she should never have come back to the flat. She didn't know why she had. 'I have to go,' she announced abruptly. 'Give Eva my love when you see her.'

Michael saw her out, and she hurried away without looking back.

Closing her own front door, she leaned back against it for a minute. Her breathlessness was *not* from hurrying across the corridor. She must not, ever, see him again.

She stared at the flowers he'd bought, and walked slowly across to gently finger the petals. It's an interlude, Kerith, that's all. Don't read more into it than there is. No. Right.

Walking briskly into the kitchen, she switched on the kettle, and then switched it off. She didn't want tea. Nor coffee.

She didn't see them the next day. She assumed they'd gone out to see Eva. She watered her plants, even gave their leaves a shine, and then began on the ironing, and couldn't stop thinking about him. About his smile. The way his eyes lit up from within. His long-fingered, expressive, hands—and the fact that he'd called her eminently kissable.

The man's a flirt, Kerith. Yes. He'd flirted with the checkout girl at the store. Well, maybe not *flirted* with her, but he'd made her laugh. Mr Cheerer Upper. Mr Amusement.

Monday was no better. Distracted and therefore inefficient, which she hated, she got thoroughly fed up with her colleagues asking her if something was wrong; or teasing her for her inattention, her obvious daydreaming. Asking if she was in love. 'Don't be ridiculous!' she'd snapped. Of course she wasn't in love. She was worried about Eva. About Michael. It had absolutely nothing to do with a man with blue eyes.

Parking her car, her face as grumpy as her thoughts, she shoved her key into the outer door of the flats and then halted as a familiar, becoming far *too* familiar, voice shouted her name from behind her. Felt her body stiffen, as it always seemed to stiffen when she was near him.

Cautiously turning, she watched Tris loping through the entryway. He looked ridiculous. No, he didn't.

'I saw you drive in.'

Forcing herself into abruptness, because abruptness was safer, she demanded, 'And?'

'And I needed to catch up with you,' he said with a smile. 'I don't have a key to the outer door.'

'Then, how did you get in before?'

'By trading on people's good natures.'

Yes, she could believe that. People would be only too *pleased* to help him out.

Opening the door, she let him in. 'I have a spare key you can borrow,' she said quietly. 'You can let me have it back when you leave.'

'Yes, ma'am.'

She gave him a look that she hoped was derisive.

'Did you go to see Eva?' she asked as they climbed the stairs side by side.

'Yes.'

'How is she?'

'Not too bad. She'll probably fly home at the end of next week.'

She nodded.

He held the top door open for her, then followed her along the corridor. They both halted outside Eva's flat.

Ridiculously conscious of him behind her, she turned to face him—only to find him much too close.

He cleared his throat. A scratchy little sound that forced her eyes to his mouth. What *would* it be like to kiss him?

'Michael's playing with a neighbour of Lena's. He's the same age. They're building a tree house.'

'Oh,' she murmured inadequately as she continued to stare at his lips. 'You didn't want to stay and help?' she whispered and then forced herself into sensibility before he noticed her odd behaviour. Forced herself to look into his eyes. Blue eyes, the colour of summer skies. Such beautiful eyes, laughing eyes.

'No.'

'And you don't usually stay in England whilst Michael is here, do you?'

He shook his head.

Then, why now, she wanted to ask, but didn't. 'Doesn't Michael have to go back to school?'

'Not for a while yet—two weeks on Wednesday, I think!

'And you're staying—here?'

'Mmm,' he agreed.

Perhaps he couldn't afford to stay anywhere else. All this toing and froing across the Channel, to Greece, must be expensive.

'Don't tell Eva will you?'

She continued to stare at him, then gave an impatient little shake of her head. 'Because she wouldn't like you staying here?'

He gave a rueful little smile. 'No.'

'All right,' she agreed, 'I won't tell her, but...'

'I should really go somewhere else?'

'No, but I won't lie if she asks me.'

'I would never ask you to lie, Kerith.'

Wouldn't he? she wondered. But what else might he ask her to do? She turned quickly away. 'I have to go. I'll get you that key.'

He followed her along to her flat.

'What are you having for dinner?'

'I didn't invite you,' she said without turning.

'I know you didn't. I was asking you out.'

'No, thanks,' she said, turning him down.

She knew he smiled. Absolutely *knew*. Because he was acting. No, he *wasn't*.

'Then, tell me where to go.'

'Don't tempt me,' she said under her breath, but he heard. Of course he heard. Uncomfortable, twitchy, she quickly opened her door. 'There are several restaurants in the High Street,' she informed him. 'I have no idea which is best.'

'But I don't like eating alone.'

'Tough.'

He gave a muffled chuckle that stirred the hairs on the back of her neck.

'Hard lady.'

Trying to be, she wanted to say. Trying.

He waited outside whilst she went inside to get the key and when she returned and handed it to him he tossed it lightly in his palm for a moment before putting it in his pocket. 'Thank you.'

'Don't forget to give it me back.'

'I won't. When's your next auction?' he asked idly as he gently tucked a strand of her thick hair back into place.

She shivered and stepped back. 'Why do you want to know?' she asked suspiciously.

'No reason, just making conversation.'

Needing to get away from him, needing space, she held the door like a barrier. 'Stop hovering.'

'Sorry, I'm not used to being at a loose end.'

'No, I don't imagine you are. I imagine women fall all over themselves in order to tie *up* your loose ends.'

He laughed. 'I wish. Stopped disliking me, Kerith?' he asked gently.

'I don't know. Now go away.'

He gave a small smile. 'You could shut the door in my face.'

'Don't think I won't.'

His eyes creased in amusement. 'Are you a good auctioneer?' he asked softly.

'Yes.'

'Yes,' he agreed even more softly. 'I imagine you are efficient at whatever you do.'

'I'm not being very efficient at getting rid of you, am I?'

He laughed. 'Enjoy your evening.' Turning, he walked away and, finally, she was able to close the door. She would do better not to see him again.

She saw him the next evening. He was on the stairs talking to the lady who lived above them when she returned home. And she was pleased to see him. Felt a little leap of happiness that really rather worried her. Being attracted to Tris Jensen was a waste of emotion. It wasn't going anywhere. It couldn't. He lived in France. She lived in England. And he would never remarry. He'd said so. Anyway, she didn't want to marry him. She didn't want to live in France. She wanted to be independent, secure, safe. Boring.

Mrs Davies gave her a wide smile. 'The very person we need!' she exclaimed. 'We were just talking about you.'

'Something nice I hope,' she returned and kept her eyes very firmly away from Tris.

'Of course something nice, I doubt anyone could find anything nasty to say about you. Or you to them.'

'Puce shirt,' Tris muttered under his breath and she had to bite her lip.

'What was that, dear?'

He shook his head.

'Oh, well, as I was saying, if anyone would know, you would.'

Bewildered, Kerith asked, 'Know what?'

'Nothing,' Tris put in, that appealing laughter in the back of his eyes. 'Really, it's nothing.'

'Now, that's foolish Mr Jensen. Kerith won't mind you asking her. She's very kind like that.' She suddenly stilled, cocked her head to one side. 'Is that my phone? Yes, I think it is.' With a last smile, she hurried up the remaining stairs and left Tris and Kerith alone on the landing.

'Are you?' he asked softly.

'Am I what?' she asked without looking at him.

'Kind like that?'

'No,' she denied automatically. 'What were you going to ask me?'

'Nothing.'

'Tris...' she warned.

'Truly. I really wasn't going to ask you. I've asked enough of late.'

Yes, he had. More than he knew. Pushing open the door which led to their flats she walked with him down the corridor and halted outside Eva's door. 'What is it you wanted?'

A small indent appeared at the corner of his mouth as though he were trying very hard not to laugh. 'I can't get the washing machine to work.'

She just stared at him. 'I don't believe you. You flew round the *world*!'

'I had a manual.'

Her lips twitched and she hastily straightened them. 'If you're lying…?'

'Why would I lie?'

Yes, why would he? Looking away from him, she indicated for him to open the door.

He led the way inside as he continued, 'I've tried every combination known to man. Why can't they just have a start button?'

'I don't know. Because they were designed by men I expect.' He smiled. She knew he did, even without being able to see his face, she knew.

'Busy day at work?' he asked sympathetically as he led the way into the kitchen.

'Yes,' she agreed. Not that it had been any busier than usual, but it was an excuse for her odd behaviour, wasn't it?

The door swung silently to behind them, and she

remembered, too late, that Eva's kitchen wasn't like hers. It was a great deal smaller. There was barely room to swing a cat which meant that he was now closer to her than he'd ever been before, which meant she would have to pass him in the narrow space, and the air suddenly felt charged, electrical. To her. It didn't seem to be affecting him. Squeezing past, she stood in front of the machine. 'Is it loaded?'

'Yes.'

'With?'

When he didn't immediately answer, she turned to stare at him. A stare of defiance for the unwanted intimacy.

'You have the most amazing eyes,' he said softly.

'Don't,' she said thickly.

'No.'

Feeling panicky because this was going too far too fast, because she no longer felt in control of her life, because she didn't know how to *respond*, she demanded 'So what have you loaded it with?'

He looked confused.

'Cotton? Wool?' she prompted impatiently. 'Delicates…'

'Oh, underwear mostly, a couple of shirts, bedclothes, towels.'

'All the same colour?'

He frowned, even though his eyes were still on hers, then shook his head.

Mouth tight, because it was the only way she could cope, she dumped her bag on the counter and bent to unload the machine. Sorting everything into colour, she checked the fabrics, then reloaded. He had nice underwear, she couldn't help noticing. Furious with herself, with him, because this really would not do, she checked the soap dispenser, filled it, then twisted the dial on the front of the machine and switched it on. 'When it's finished, in about an hour, everything should be dry. It's a washer-drier, and if you fold everything properly, hang your shirts on hangers, with a bit of luck they won't need ironing. All the rest will go on number four, put in more soap powder, and you press this little button here to restart it. OK?' she asked without looking at him.

'Yes. Number four. Thank you.'

Aware of him in a way she didn't want to be aware, she picked up her bag.

'And, um…'

She looked at him, almost daring him to do something, say something.

He gave an apologetic smile. It didn't look real. It looked distracted, absent, as though his mind were somewhere else. 'The dishwasher? I filled the salt dispenser, put the powder in but, for the life of me, I can't discover how to switch it on.'

She knew everyone had different models, and they *were* difficult to figure out sometimes, and with anyone else she would have been pleased to help, not make it seem as though it was a *chore*. But with this man, who she couldn't stop thinking about, who was disrupting her life...

With a deep sigh, she put her bag back down and bent to check that it was loaded properly. 'You almost close the door,' she explained, 'depress the end button here...' He leaned over her to see what she was doing, and she felt stifled, trapped. Distancing her mind, *determinedly* distancing her mind, her emotions, she continued in a voice she barely recognised as her own, 'And then, when you hear it start, you close the door properly. But don't use it until the washing machine is finished otherwise the water all backs up and you'll have a flood. The pipe can't cope with two lots of water shooshing through it at the same time.' Or that was what the plumber had said when she'd had the same problem.

'Thank you.'

Just wanting to *go*, she grabbed for her bag, missed the strap, and upended the contents all over the floor. They both dropped down to pick them up at the same time and, in her haste not to touch him, have him touch her, she jerked back—and yelped in pain as her hair got caught on one of his buttons. Frightened, she tried to wrench free.

'Don't!' he said urgently as he caught her head to hold it still. 'You'll end up with a bald patch if you do that! Keep still.'

Unbearably conscious of his chest only an inch

from her cheek, of his hands gently trying to untangle her hair, and seemingly totally unable to regulate her breathing that was all out of control, she froze. This was ridiculous. Utterly and stupidly ridiculous.

'Nearly there,' he said quietly, and his voice sounded odd—strained—as his fingers touched, and retouched her head, her face. She could feel his breath against her, see the rise and fall of his chest, and she wanted—to be out of there, she told herself frantically. Unable to bear it any longer, she moved her head.

'Kerith!' he snapped almost angrily. 'Keep still!'

'I can't!' As she crouched, hunched awkwardly over, her legs were beginning to tremble with the effort to stay in one position, and she didn't know where to put her arms. Her shoulders ached, her chest felt cramped—and then she was free.

'There.'

'Thank you,' she muttered. She straightened and found there was nowhere to step back out of his way.

He reached out to gently untangle the hair he'd just released, and she slapped his hand away.

'Don't! I have to go! Will you please get out of my *way*?'

'Kerith...'

She stared at him. He stared at her, and the air seemed too thick to breathe.

'No,' she denied in renewed panic.

'No,' he agreed. But he kissed her anyway. She didn't fight, just closed her eyes—and then pushed him violently away before she could succumb.

CHAPTER FOUR

'I'M SORRY,' he apologised gently. 'I shouldn't have done that.'

'No, you shouldn't,' she said breathlessly, raggedly. 'So just stay away from me, Tris Jensen. Just stay away. And don't be *nice* to me!' she ordered. Scrabbling all her belongings into her bag, she forced herself past him and ran out. And then couldn't get into her flat.

Angry, frustrated, *furious*, she rummaged frantically in her bag for her keys. They weren't there. She must have left them on his kitchen floor. And she couldn't go back. She couldn't.

With some half-baked ideas that she would go down to her car, drive around until she felt calmer, find the *janitor*, she turned and saw Tris watching her. He held her keys in his hand.

He didn't say anything, just looked at her with sympathy and kindness, and that made it all ten times worse. He walked across the landing, opened her door and ushered her inside.

'Go and sit down,' he ordered gently.

Too tired and embarrassed to argue, she slumped in the armchair. 'I don't *want* this,' she said fiercely. 'It has taken me *years* to get where I am. Months of work, effort, exams, sacrificing my social life, striving towards—excellence! And I won't, *won't*, be distracted by blue eyes and a winning smile!'

'No,' he agreed gently.

She heard him go into the kitchen, heard the soft hum as the kettle began to boil and she gave a small, humourless, smile. Tea, the panacea for all ills. But not this one. And how, how, she asked herself despairingly, could it all have come to this? She had *known* not to be attracted to him. Had told herself a hundred million times not to get involved. She couldn't *afford* distractions. Of any kind! It was *vital* she get her next set of exams. Vital she get the job she'd been offered if she passed.

Perhaps she took after her mother. Perhaps there was something in their genes that made them fall for a certain type of man. Not that she'd *fallen* for him. But she was attracted, she admitted honestly. She didn't want to be, had tried so very hard not to be because it wouldn't work, it couldn't work. And when he'd kissed her—she hadn't known how to respond. And she'd wanted to. *That* was what was chewing her up. Her lack of experience. Her *embarrassment* at not knowing what to do.

She heard his soft entrance, and looked defiantly up. Searched his face. He looked—concerned.

He hooked a small table over with his foot and put the cup he was carrying carefully down.

'I'm sorry,' she blurted again. 'I just…'

'Have been doing too much,' he completed for her.

'Yes,' she agreed gratefully. Unable to look at him, she reached out for the cup and cradled it in her palms. Her hands were shaking. 'I'm all right now.'

'Have you eaten today?'

She gave a small, bitter, smile. If only it was as simple as not eating. 'I had a sandwich at lunchtime,' she managed to say.

'Which isn't enough,' he reproved, 'when you're working all day. May I use your phone?'

'Sure.' Not really interested in why he wanted it, or who he was calling, she watched him as he stood with his back to her. So tall. All arms and legs and a broad back. His hair was attractively ruffled as though he'd been running his fingers through it. Perhaps he had. Or, perhaps she had. She didn't remember.

His jeans were snug over his hips and bottom. And she wanted him. Wanted to be held by him. Comforted. Would it be so wrong? So terrible? No, but she didn't have time for this. She had promised herself she would get her career settled first before finding—love.

He only *kissed* you, Kerith! So what on earth are you getting in such a state about? *Was* he attracted? How did you tell? How did you really *know*? She was in danger of making a fool of herself. Reading too much into it. But she did wonder, just for a moment, if she hadn't been throwing the baby out with the bath water. She kept telling herself that her career was all, which it had been. Until now.

He made her dream dreams, dreams she'd always suppressed. But she couldn't shrug off her past, her upbringing, become a cap-over-the-windmill sort of girl. She wasn't ready to settle down. And when she was, well, she'd need someone who lived where she did, not in another country.

And now he would think she was some sort of moron. But she had to be in control. She *always* had to be in control, otherwise things would sneak up on her, messing things up.

How many other women had there been? Women who had wanted him? A great many according to Eva.

Was he used to this? Women falling apart at the seams when he was near? Did he give them all tea? Sympathy? A smiling face and a careless heart, is that what he was? He must know how she felt, must have seen it all before. So why had he kissed her? Because he felt the same way? She doubted it. He'd kissed her on impulse, because she was there.

She should get up, tell him she was all right now, see him out. But she felt too tired. Too worried. Why couldn't she be like other girls? Give in to it? Enjoy it? Have fun? Because she couldn't. Because she wasn't like that.

He replaced the receiver and turned to face her. 'Bath,' he said softly.

'What?' she asked in confusion.

'Bath.' He walked out into the small hall and she heard him open the bathroom door. Heard the tap running. Together? she wondered in alarm. No, surely not—and then wondered what it would be like to bath with him. Erotic, she imagined.

Finishing her tea, she shakily replaced the cup on the saucer. She wouldn't think about it any more.

'Bath's ready,' he said softly and she snapped open her eyes in shock. She'd almost fallen asleep. 'You have an hour.'

'An hour?' she echoed stupidly.

'Mmm,' he agreed.

'It doesn't take an hour to have a bath!'

'It does if you're having a nice soak. Go.' He held out his hand to help her up and she put her own into it. The first time she had touched him voluntarily. She felt his warm palm against her own.

He opened the bathroom door for her, and she walked bemusedly inside. The curtain had been drawn across the window to shut out the dying light and four candles glittered merrily along the vanity unit scenting the steamy air with magnolia. Someone had bought them for her last Christmas and they had lain ever since, unused, in the small cupboard under the sink. Bubbles frothed the surface of the water. Another Christmas present that had never been used.

'Don't let the water get cold,' he warned softly from behind her and then closed the door.

Slowly undressing, she tested the water, then climbed in, and she couldn't believe how luxurious it felt. How soothing. Lying back, she stared at the wavering candles and then closed her eyes—only to open them again when soft music began to play outside the door. He surely hadn't moved the stereo?

How disastrous would it be to have an affair with him? She did not know, but it would probably be exciting and wonderful. Short-lived? And why are you even *thinking* this, Kerith? You don't have time for an affair. And probably all he was thinking was how he could get out of there! He must think she'd run mad. Just because a man kisses you doesn't mean he wants an affair.

With a dispirited sigh, she poked her toes up through the bubbles and stared at them. She had nice toes. With a brief, unamused, laugh, she lay her head back, began to feel pampered, and lazy, and sort of yearning.

Had he run baths like this for his wife? For other girls? Men like Tris liked to please women, but being looked after, cared for, was only one side of the coin. The other side was—what? She didn't know, because she didn't know *him*. And wanted to. Romance had been sacrificed along with friends, and for what? You know for what, she told herself determinedly.

He'd confused her, that was all, because it had happened so fast. That was the trouble. Innately cautious, she wasn't used to fast. Be honest, Kerith, you aren't used to anything to do with men. She always shied away, told herself her career was all. Because of her mother. Yes.

Warned off boys at an early age, an age when girls learned to flirt and tease, her mother had become hysterical if she'd even smiled at a boy. Anyway, boys had always thought her snooty.

With a sigh, she closed her eyes again, gave in to the pleasure of a warm bath. A pleasure she had almost forgotten. Always busy, always in a rush, she hadn't had a bath in a very long time. She always showered. It was quicker. How long since she'd stopped to count the daisies? Or whatever the expression was. She had thought herself happy with her busy lifestyle. Contented. Continually told herself that, anyway. Until she'd met Tris. And it wouldn't work. He wouldn't move to England, couldn't, because of Michael's schooling. And she couldn't, wouldn't, move to France. Even if he asked her, which wasn't likely. If she had learned nothing else from her life, she had learned that she needed to be independent. Have her own money, her own security. She didn't think she could ever be wholly dependent on a man, couldn't bear to have to ask for money for tights, or make-up or shoes. She could remember her mother doing it. Could clearly remember the humiliation on her face.

But it needn't be like that. Not with the right man.

You're repressed, Kerith, she told herself gloomily. Yes, but then she already knew that, didn't she?

She opened her eyes and stared at the candles. They had an almost memerising effect. Made her feel sleepy. But she mustn't go to sleep.

Eyelids heavy, she allowed them to drop, felt herself begin to drift, and didn't care. This was bliss. Heavenly bliss. The scent of the candles, the bubbles, and she could dream, couldn't she? About the man in her flat.

The rap on the door woke her with a start.

'Don't go to sleep,' Tris called.

She mumbled something and forced herself awake. Blinking rapidly to try and get some energy back into her body, and realising that the water was cooling, she climbed reluctantly out. Her hair was soaking at the back where she'd slid down in the bath and so she rubbed it as dry as she could before shrugging into her dressing gown that was hanging behind the door.

She blew out the candles one by one, emptied the bath, and walked across to her bedroom. Her face in the mirror looked the same, a little sleepy maybe, but basically the same. A cloud of dark hair and grey-green eyes. She didn't *feel* the same, but that was how she looked. She cleaned her face and moisturised it and then, for a reason she didn't bother to analyse, she found the lounging pyjamas that her mother had bought her a long time ago and which she had never worn. Pulling them on, she dragged a brush through her hair and, as she padded out in her bare feet, she saw her small radio sitting by the bathroom door. The source of the music.

Did such thoughtful gestures come naturally to him? Or was it only because it was for her? Because he cared?

Walking into the lounge, she halted. Her foldaway table had been pulled out and laid with her best china and glasses. Her red Christmas candle, still with the holly round its base and dried wax clumping its sides, sat in the middle.

Tris was standing at the window, looking out. Maybe he saw her reflexion in the glass, or maybe he heard her come in; whatever, he turned. He didn't smile, just watched her and her words tumbled out before she could stop them.

'Have there been a lot of women, Tris?'

He didn't seem surprised by her question, nor angry. 'No,' he denied simply.

'And you don't want a serious relationship, or marriage, or anything, do you?'

'No.'

'Why?'

He shook his head. 'Dinner won't be long.'

She gave a sadly wry smile. She'd been beating herself up over it and he didn't want anything to do with her. 'Dinner?' She looked towards the kitchen where there were certainly no sounds of cooking, nor even smells, and glanced back at him in puzzlement.

'It's being delivered.'

'Oh.'

'Feeling better?'

'Yes. Thank you. I'm sorry for my earlier behaviour.'

'You don't need to apologise for me,' he reproved gently.

'Yes, I do. I behaved like an idiot.'

'No, that was me. Heart and head are having a bit of a disagreement at the moment. I shouldn't have kissed you. I shouldn't even be here.'

'Why?'

He shook his head. 'Unfair not to tell you, I know, but it really is better this way.'

'Yes,' she agreed, because it was. Maybe. 'I didn't want to be attracted to you,' she said simply, then gave an embarrassed grimace. 'I shouldn't say that, should I? I don't always think before I speak. A bit of a blurter,' she added, trying to summon another smile. 'Very career-minded. I have the chance of being promoted, working for a top London firm. It's what I've wanted, worked for, and I don't have affairs,' she completed quickly.

'I didn't ask for an affair.'

'I know. I'm just explaining why I—panicked. I thought at first that you were like my father...' Now, why on earth had she mentioned that?

'But, I'm not?'

'No. And yet it was my father who helped to shape me, make me what I am. Determined, cautious, in need of security. Because of his fickle ways, his leaving me and my mother with no money and, in my mother's case, no self-respect, I swore I would never put myself in that position again.' Shut up, Kerith, shut up.

'You don't have to tell me all this,' he said gently.

'No, I know, and you don't really forget Michael's birthdays, do you? Or his school fees?'

He looked puzzled. 'No.'

'No,' she agreed. 'I don't know about men, Tris,' she stated with rather endearing simplicity. 'About what they want or mean. You can go if you like, you don't have to stay.'

'I'll stay.'

'Then, I'll try not to embarrass you any more.'

'You haven't embarrassed me.' He smiled, and she managed a more relaxed smile back.

There was tension between them, a thin, scratchy, tension, which both would ignore. Because it was better. Because she'd made a fool of herself. She might look confident and assured, which she was in her job, in her life, but not with things personal. And now she had to tough it out, be brave.

Walking across to the table, she rested her hands on one of the chair backs. 'The table looks nice,' she said with an effort. 'I don't usually bother.'

'Then, you should. Eating off your knees in front of the television is very bad for your digestion. Meals should be savoured, enjoyed, not eaten on the hop.'

She gave another small smile. 'That sounds very French.'

'No,' he denied, 'it sounds very sensible.'

'And I suppose you never eat on the hop, as you put it?' she asked drily.

'That's better,' he approved. 'Feisty I can cope with—and, yes, I do. More often than I should.' Faint humour in his eyes, he stated softly. 'You said I reminded you of your father. Did he wear puce?'

'Puce...' she began in puzzlement, and then laughed. 'No.'

'But we look alike?'

She shook her head. 'He was shorter, and dark.'

'Still alive?'

'No, he died a few years ago. I—' The doorbell rang and she broke off relieved that she didn't have to explain.

He answered the door and a few minutes later she watched him walk into the kitchen carrying several foil containers.

He brought in a bowl of salad and a bottle of red wine, followed by lasagne which he'd dished up onto two of her plates.

'Tuck in,' he urged her.

They sat on opposite sides of the table, each aware of the other, each silent with their own thoughts. Hers were composed of wanting and denial. She didn't know what his were. He looked slightly sombre, she thought, when she risked a quick glance. Thoughtful. Sad.

She didn't want to rush into speech any more, wished she hadn't in the first place, didn't want to break this fragile mood but normality had to be pretended, didn't it? And so they talked briefly, quietly, about Eva's injuries, about Michael, about France, but nothing controversial—nor threatening. He had a gentle, self-deprecating humour, that made her smile, and she liked him. Was quite possibly falling in love with him. Or not. She didn't know very much about love. But this was probably the last time they would meet. He would return to his life. She to hers.

The lasagne finished, he raised his glass to her. 'To a very beautiful companion.'

'Thank you,' she said awkwardly.

'Tell me about auctioneering,' he ordered softly.

And so she told him, briefly, about the excitement of finding something valuable, something that had maybe been hidden away in someone's attic. About the buzz she got when an auction went well and they made a nice profit.

'How often do you have them?'

'Once a month. We try to specialise if we have enough stock. Furniture one month, then pottery, books.'

'A lot of dealers?'

'A fair number, but the nice thing is not everyone wants something valuable to be polished and cleaned and never used.' With a small smile, she added, 'It never ceases to amaze me the things people buy.'

'One man's meat is another man's poison?'

'Yes.'

'And when's the next auction?'

'This Friday. Rather a mishmash this month. Not enough of any one type for exclusivity.'

'And so you have to be a jack of all trades?'

'Sometimes. We have a great many experts we can call on if we need help in dating something of course, or valuing it. I saw some *really* nice pieces when I was in France.'

He smiled. 'Yes, I think I almost furnished my entire house from flea markets.'

'Michael said it was nice.'

He laughed, gave rather a rueful grimace. 'It will be. And now it's time to say goodnight.'

She looked down, gave a pensive sigh. 'Yes, I

have a busy day tomorrow. It's preview day,' she explained when he gave her a querying glance.

'Yes, of course.' Getting to his feet, he began clearing the table. She got up to help him.

The containers were rinsed and thrown into the bin, the plates and glasses stacked in the dishwasher and, when all was tidy again, he looked at her—and then walked slowly towards the front door. 'Goodbye, Kerith.'

'Goodbye,' she whispered.

He gave a last, strained smile and stepped out into the corridor. 'It wouldn't work,' he said with his back to her.

'No,' she agreed.

She slowly closed the door. No, it probably wouldn't have worked. He was a nice man. A kind man. A very attractive, charming, man. Who lived in France.

But why did *he* think it wouldn't work? She would like to have known that.

She didn't see him the next day and she felt deprived. He was in her mind. Her heart. And she didn't know how to deal with it.

On Friday morning, because it was auction day, and because she needed to be smart, she dressed in a dark grey suit, high heels, a slick of mascara, blusher and lipstick. Miss Executive, she taunted herself as she gave her appearance a last glance before leaving.

Still troubled by her feelings for Tris, she drove to work, parked, took a deep breath to calm the nerves that always affected her before she took her place on the podium, and became the professional she truly was.

There was a good turnout, which meant her boss would be pleased, which, in turn, made life easier for the rest of them. Taking her place, she surveyed the crowd, and indicated for the first item to be brought.

Two hours later, with only a few items remaining, the bidding going well on a Royal Doulton figure, she suddenly saw Tris at the back of the hall and faltered. Snapping her eyes away from him, conscious of the whispers and restless shifting of the crowd, she quickly pulled herself together.

'I'm sorry,' she apologised, 'I believe the bidding was with you, sir.' The porter who was holding the figurine quickly whispered the amount they'd reached and the bidding resumed.

Angry with herself for being distracted, she forced herself to concentrate on the next few items and then thankfully laid down her gavel.

She thanked the porter as she stepped down and he laughed and said it was nice to know she was human after all, which surprised her.

'Of course I'm human,' she said with a frown.

'I know.' He grinned. 'But you make the rest of us look second-rate.'

'Rubbish.' Still frowning, she asked hesitantly, 'Is that what you all think of me? That I'm...'

'The best?'

'No! That I'm , well, that I somehow think myself superior?'

'No,' he denied softly, 'that *we* do—and, oh...' he smiled '...how we fantasise. Go and get your coffee.'

Fantasise? Walking slowly away, still preoccupied by the porter's words, she pushed through the rear door.

'Stop beating yourself up,' Sheila, a female colleague, teased. 'It happens to us all. And *I* would have lost the plot if he'd suddenly appeared in my line of vision.'

'What?'

'The tall hunk at the back. Now *that* is sexy. Who is he?'

'No one,' she denied absently.

The outer door creaked open and both girls whirled round to find Tris leaning negligently inside the outer door.

Her heart skipped a beat, and she found it almost impossible to drag her eyes away from his. 'You aren't supposed to be in here,' Kerith said crossly. 'It's for staff only.'

'Then, come out here.'

She didn't know why she went. Had no idea at

all why she meekly followed him outside. It was over. He'd said so. Over before it had begun.

'I wanted to apologise,' he said quietly. 'I didn't mean to put you off your stroke.'

'You shouldn't have been able to. What are you doing here, anyway?'

'Being nosy,' he confessed. 'I wanted to see you in your own environment.'

She looked quickly away. That was what she wanted: to see him in his. And if he wanted the same, then... Snapping her eyes back to his she searched his face, his eyes, and saw nothing to comfort. Sheila would have known how to interpret his words, what to do, say.

Wishing she were Sheila, fighting down her attraction, an attraction that was becoming more and more alarming as each day passed, she asked huskily, 'You just happened to be passing?'

'Mmm.'

She didn't believe him. 'How did you know where I worked?'

'Michael. We were going past one day and he happened to mention it.'

'I see.'

The door behind her thudded into her heels and she moved quickly away as her colleague emerged. 'I brought you your coffee,' she informed Kerith brightly. 'Would you like one?' she asked Tris.

'No, thanks.' He smiled.

With an irritated sigh, Kerith introduced them. 'Sheila, this is Tris. Tris, Sheila, a colleague of mine.'

They shook hands. Sheila looked as though all her dreams had come true at once. An outrageous flirt, she batted her eyelashes at him, and he laughed.

'Available?' she asked him.

'For what?'

'*Anything*!' she exclaimed.

With a disgusted snort, Kerith went back inside.

Sheila was still missing over an hour later. What on earth were they finding to talk about?

When Sheila finally did return, she was wearing a smile as wide as the Cheddar Gorge.

'I think I'm in love!' she exclaimed happily. 'Not treading on your toes am I?' she asked Kerith.

'No,' she denied grumpily. 'And Max is looking for you.'

She smiled. 'I could even cope with our revered boss at this moment. I feel entirely revived. I've had my lunch, by the way, so if you want to go and have yours...' With a last smile, she drifted away.

Had lunch with Tris? Kerith wondered. Presumably so. Not that she cared, she told herself. Not that it was any of her business. He was a free agent. So was Sheila.

She wondered if they were seeing each other again.

She spent the rest of the day in something of a daze. She kept imagining them together, laughing, joking, Tris flirting... But Eva would be back on Monday and Tris would return to France. Once he was gone, it would be easy to forget. And avoidance, until he left, would be even better, she decided. She would spend the weekend with her mother.

Her mother didn't want her either, as it turned out, and Kerith gave a wry smile.

'It isn't *funny*, Kerith!'

'No,' she agreed, which it wasn't.

'You don't usually turn up without notice. You're very welcome, of course, but it's far too late for me to get someone to take my place at work.'

'I don't want someone to take your place. Go,' Kerith ordered. 'I shall be quite happy to potter.'

Her mother gave an aggrieved sigh. 'I suppose I could call in sick.'

'I don't want you to call in sick.' In truth, she would be far happier left to her own devices. 'Go,' she persuaded again.

Her mother looked indecisive for a moment, her face set in the familiar sour expression, and Kerith gave a mental sigh. They were never going to get on, never be friends, and that was sad. 'What were you like...?' Breaking off, she shook her head. She couldn't really ask her what she'd been like before she'd met her father. 'Go on, off you go. I'll see you later.' Dropping a swift kiss on her mother's lined cheek, she stepped inside and her mother left, her back as angry and stiff as it always was.

What *had* she been like? Kerith wondered. Happy? Laughing? In love? She hadn't been like that by the time Kerith had been old enough to remember. Her memories of childhood were of a stern woman, tight-lipped. Always complaining, angry about something or another. Her father had been charming, always laughing, pulling faces, teasing her, siding with her against his wife's complaining. 'Tidy your bedroom', 'Do your homework'—never said in an encouraging way, but always with a sort of despairing anger.

What made people the way they were? Circumstances? Genes? What had made her father into a charming philanderer? He must have loved her mother once, or else why marry her? Maybe he'd had to.

Her face thoughtful, she walked slowly upstairs and into her mother's bedroom where the twin beds still sat on either side of the room. Opening the wardrobe, she bent to take out the photograph albums. Seated cross-legged on the floor, she went through them. Every picture of her father had been removed. Some photographs had been torn in half leaving just her or her mother and a jagged edge. And neither of them ever seemed to wear happy faces. There were very few of Kerith laughing, or even smiling. She looked wary, she thought. A mass of dark hair and a solemn face. But always immaculate. There weren't any of her playing with mud, nor getting dirty.

Sad beyond measure, she replaced them. And yet, she didn't remember her early childhood being unhappy. She did remember siding with her father against her mother. She could clearly remember pulling faces with him behind her mother's back. How awful. And yet, to a child, it had all seemed normal. She hadn't liked her mother very much— because her father had promoted such feelings?

Sorely troubled, she went downstairs to make herself something to eat. When her mother returned home from her voluntary work at the local hospital—something that had always amused Kerith, until now, because her mother looked like the last woman to bring comfort to others—Kerith was deadheading the last of the roses in the small back garden.

Her mother didn't thank her, merely said shortly, and somehow accusingly, 'I was going to do that later.'

'Sorry,' Kerith murmured. 'Want a cup of tea?'

'I can make it,' she said abruptly.

With a long sigh, she replaced the secateurs in the shed, the very neat and tidy shed, and walked slowly back to the kitchen. Which she had left as pristine as she'd found it.

Seating herself at the small kitchen table, she watched her mother make the tea. Her fair hair had quite a few silver threads, she saw. The face very lined for a woman only in her early fifties.

'Did you always hate me?' Kerith asked quietly.

Obviously shocked, her mother whirled round. 'I don't hate you!'

'Well, maybe not hate,' she qualified, 'but you don't like me very much, do you?'

She didn't answer, merely turned back to fuss with the cups.

'Didn't you want a baby?'

'Yes,' she snapped shortly.

'But?'

'We weren't married,' she admitted harshly.

'Oh. But he did marry you when he found out.'

She gave a derisive laugh. 'Only because his parents forced him into it. I sometimes wish they hadn't. He sulked for days. We didn't even have a honeymoon. But I thought, once you were born…' She sighed again. 'It spoilt it all, you see. And the only time he paid any attention to you when you were a baby was when someone else was there. The proud father,' she scoffed. Carrying the tea over to the table, pot, milk jug, sugar bowl, as though she were entertaining, she sat down and began to pour. 'There was never much money.'

'But he had a good job, didn't he?'

'Yes, he worked in advertising, but he liked to—entertain. I didn't hate you Kerith.'

'But if you hadn't had me, he would have stayed his charming self?'

'Maybe. Or I would have got over him, married someone else.' With a bitter smile, she added, 'The trouble was, I loved him. Oh, I knew what he was like, knew his faults, his weaknesses, but I loved him.'

'And I thought he loved me,' Kerith said sadly.

'He did. When you were old enough to be interesting, he adored you. You were such a beautiful child, like Snow White. That's what he called you. His little Snow White. He did love you Kerith.'

But he wouldn't have done if she'd been plain? 'As he must have loved you,' she murmured. 'He stayed with you for fifteen years.'

She gave another bitter laugh. 'Don't be a fool. He liked the *fact* of being married. He could flirt, seduce, and if anyone got heavy, he would say "Sorry, but you knew I was married."'

'He had a lot of affairs?'

'Oh, yes.'

'And he knew that you knew?'

'He made sure that I did.'

'And I always took his side, didn't I?'

'Yes.'

'I'm sorry. Why did he go when he did?' she asked curiously.

'I don't know. I went shopping and when I came back he'd packed up all his things and gone. No note, no nothing. His parents didn't know where he was. Neither did his friends. He just—went.'

And she'd blamed her mother. All her teenage years had been spent in hate—and avoidance of boys. 'I'm sorry.'

'No,' her mother said. 'I'm the one who should be sorry. I should have explained.'

She gave a wry smile. 'I doubt I would have believed you.'

'No. And the terrible thing is, if he hadn't died, if he walked through that door right now, I would forgive him. I would hate myself, but I would forgive him.'

Looking up, she stared at her daughter. 'You look like him,' she stated quietly. 'Apart from the colour of your eyes, you are the image of him.'

'Without the charm,' Kerith put in.

'Without the *obvious* charm,' she corrected. 'You've grown into a very beautiful woman. Elegant and assured. Don't make the mistakes I made. Use your head, Kerith, not your heart.'

Remembering a man with blue eyes and a charming smile, whose own heart and head, he'd said, were in conflict, she nodded. She was trying, but it was hard.

CHAPTER FIVE

SHE returned home late on Sunday evening and, as she parked in the dark forecourt, she looked up to see the light on in Eva's flat. She assumed Tris would take Michael back to France in the morning. And she wouldn't see him again.

She would think about him, she knew that, probably for a very long time to come, but there was to be no involvement. They'd exchanged one, very brief, kiss, and that was all. All there would ever be.

Did he think of her? Perhaps. *Was* he attracted? She didn't even really know that. Didn't know how to interpret the signs. He would perhaps have an affair with someone else—and she wouldn't. Still sitting in her car, still staring up at the lighted window, she gave a small, sad, smile. She had *had* an affair. Short-lived, admittedly. She'd been twenty-one. He'd been twenty-two. She'd liked him, or she'd persuaded herself that she had, and she'd wanted so desperately to know what it would be like to be loved. It had lasted just over a month. He'd said she was too bossy. She had organised *everything*. From meals, to what colour his apartment should be decorated, to what he wore. Bossy. Yes. She hadn't enjoyed it. Had been glad to leave. He'd also told her she was repressed. But it hadn't been repression, it had been inexperience. He hadn't been old enough to understand, and she'd been too embarrassed to tell him he was the first. It had been awkward and messy and had rather put her off trying again.

She'd made herself go out with one or two men since, but nothing very heavy or important. Men who were safe, non-threatening. She didn't think Tris would be safe. Exciting, yes, but safe?

Had he seen Sheila over the weekend? Probably not with Michael here. Sheila wasn't bossy. With a little sigh, she reached to collect her belongings from the rear seat, turned to get out—and found Tris waiting there.

He opened her door for her and asked quietly, 'Are you all right?'

Bewildered, heart beating overfast, she nodded. 'Yes, of course.'

'I heard your car drive in ages ago and, when you didn't come up, I was worried.'

'Oh, no, I'm fine. I was just thinking.' Swinging her legs out, she stood, closed the door, locked it and set the alarm. It was nice to be worried about, she found. Comforting. But she mustn't be comforted, mustn't have anything further to do with him. The more she saw of him, the harder it would be to get over him and that wouldn't do at all. Use your head, her mother had said. And she must.

She walked slowly beside him into the flats, tried desperately to ignore the feelings he generated in her.

'They should have lights out there,' he commented as he held the inner door open for her. 'It's a mugger's paradise.'

'We haven't had any of those.'

'Yet,' he cautioned. 'Did you have a good evening?'

'I went to my mother's for the weekend.'

They climbed the stairs side by side, shoulders touching, an intimacy she didn't want. Did want, she mentally corrected, but mustn't have.

He merely nodded and, her mind on a future that looked, at the moment, rather bleak, she accompanied him automatically along to her flat. She opened the door, and then blurted, 'I could make you a coffee.'

He touched her shoulders, turned her, and looked down into her shadowed face. 'I don't want coffee,' he said quietly. 'And I promised myself I wouldn't see you again. Have you had affairs, Kerith?'

How strange that he should ask that when she'd just been thinking about it. And why had he asked it? Her eyes wide on his face, she whispered, 'One.'

'One,' he echoed sombrely and almost, it seemed, as though he wasn't in control of his own hand it lifted and he traced his fingers gently down her cheek. One knee just touched hers. His fingers moved to her hair, and she shivered, refused to move away, because she wanted this. She wanted it very much.

'I shall miss you,' he said softly. 'When I go.'

'Yes,' she managed to say. She would miss him too. There was an ache inside her, an ache that would remain unfulfilled. What would he do, say, if she told him she wanted him?

She was aware of his breathing, his warmth, his length as he stood almost against her.

'Michael in bed?' she asked desperately.

'He's still with Lena. We ring each other every day, or meet up. He can always get hold of me if he needs me. And I should go.'

'Yes.'

They continued to look at each other, still, unmoving, waiting. 'I didn't want to like you,' he said quietly, as though it mattered, as though it explained things.

'You didn't?' she asked thickly.

'No. You should never have grinned at me. Whilst we were waiting for the locksmith,' he explained. 'It was the grin that did it. It looked so happy and mischievous. Not like you at all. Not how I thought you were.' He moved his fingers from her hair to her jaw to her chin. He moved his eyes to her mouth and the ache inside turned into a pain.

'Have you been acting?' she asked thickly as she

changed the direction of her own focus. 'Laughing and smiling as though...'

'It didn't matter? Yes.'

She gave a small nod, distracted, irrelevant, as her lips parted without any advice from her brain. He had a nice mouth, nice skin and she could feel herself being drawn towards him as though invisible threads were reeling her in. She prayed they would kiss because she wanted very badly to know how it would feel. Not the brief, quick, exchange they'd had before, but a lingering, a...

She could feel her eyes closing, could feel his breath on her mouth, the increased beat of her heart, and she gave an unconscious little moan as he closed the last, tiny, gap, between them.

It was a warm kiss. Gentle and arousing, sleepy almost as he moved to lean back against the door frame and draw her against him. She put out one hand to secure herself, felt the warmth of his flesh through his shirt and curled her fingers against him.

He gently rubbed her back as he continued to kiss her and she felt drowsy and safe, warm. Excited.

She didn't know who broke the kiss, it didn't matter, but she snuggled her head into his shoulder and lay against him, her eyes closed. They didn't talk, just stood comfortably entwined. One of his legs was between hers and she could feel the strong muscles against her own. She thought she could go to sleep like this, just being held.

There was no passion to frighten or arouse, just a gentle warmth, a sort of peace.

She could feel his mouth against her hair and she stirred again, touched her lips to his throat, tasted his flesh, felt a bloom almost of pain inside.

His fingers still moved on her back, stroking, gentle, comforting and she wriggled closer, felt him stiffen slightly.

'You should go inside,' he murmured, and his voice was husky, sexy.

'Should I?'

'Yes, and you should never have become attracted to a man who wore puce.'

She gave a little chuckle and moved her head to look up at him. 'No. That was a truly revolting shirt.'

His eyes smiled down into hers. 'I bought it in the market,' he explained lazily as his fingers continued to stroke, soothe, probe. 'When I saw the disgusting state of the house I wasn't going to wear one of my good shirts to clean it up. The market was on that day, and so I bought it.'

She smiled with abstraction as she only hazily registered his words. Tracing imaginary patterns on his shirt front, she asked, 'Do you go back tomorrow?'

'I should,' he said slowly. 'That would be the right thing to do, the sensible thing to do. Eva is going to take a few days to convalesce when she comes out of hospital, and you need to go inside. Now.'

She looked up again. His eyes looked darker, the blue deeper, sending a message she *did* understand, because she wasn't a fool, and she nodded. Go now, whilst you still can.

'I shouldn't have come to your door. I knew that, but I wanted to kiss you. Totally selfish, of course, but I wanted to know how it would be.'

'Yes.' Because that was what she had wanted too. And she didn't want to leave him, leave this warmth that it had taken her twenty-eight years to discover, but she didn't have the confidence to argue, and she didn't want him to think her—desperate. It seemed to take an enormous effort to untangle herself, but she did do it, and then lingered, not wanting to say goodnight. 'I'm glad we got to be—friends,' she said softly. 'Goodnight, Tris.'

The closing of her door sounded very final.

Should, he had said. Did that mean that he would stay a few more days? She hoped so. She knew why *she* was supposed to be being sensible, but why was he? He'd said there hadn't been *many* women, but he'd presumably had affairs, so why was he being sensible with her? Because he knew her feelings weren't to be trifled with? She gave a small, sad, smile. Trifled with. It sounded so old-fashioned.

It seemed as though she didn't sleep. She supposed she must have done, but it seemed as though she was always awake, thinking about him. If he hadn't been Eva's ex-brother-in-law, if she hadn't been Eva's friend, would he have embarked on an affair with her? Seduced her? Made love to her? She didn't know. Best not to know, really. If he'd told her he was falling in love with her, then maybe things could be different. But he hadn't, and she didn't think he would. He was attracted, as was she, but love—well, love was something different, wasn't it?

He had been very gentle, very—well—solemn almost, but that didn't make it love. He would maybe remember her with affection, a smile. And she wanted to cry.

Sheila was waiting for her when she got to work the next morning.

'Hi,' she greeted Kerith casually. 'Have a good weekend?'

'Mmm, you?'

'So, so.' She followed her into the cloakroom, leaned against a basin whilst Kerith hung up her jacket and tidied her hair. 'Did you see Tris?' she asked.

'Tris? Briefly, why?'

'Oh, no reason,' she said airily.

'Did you?'

Sheila shook her head. 'I was hoping he might

phone.' Frowning, picking at a thread on her skirt, she mumbled, 'Is he married, Kerith?'

'Widowed.' Separated. She gave a little shrug, because the semantics of it didn't really matter. Only that he was—free.

'He did *say* he wouldn't phone,' she admitted honestly. 'But I sort of hoped. You know?'

Yes, she did know.

'He lives near you, doesn't he?'

'No,' she denied. Which he didn't. Not really. He *lived* in France. And she didn't want to share information with Sheila. Anyway, Tris might not want her to. 'Ready?' she asked lightly. Leading the way out to the warehouse she walked purposefully to her own desk.

The day went slowly, too slowly, but she had no reason to suppose she would see Tris that evening. Shouldn't *want* to. But she did.

'You're very quiet today.'

Looking up with a start, she smiled at the warehouseman. 'I'm always quiet.'

'Yes, but not always—preoccupied. You've been staring at that ledger without turning a page for at least half an hour. Thinking about the job offer from Pergins?'

'Pergins? Oh.' She'd almost forgotten about it. 'Yes,' she lied, and then frowned. 'You know?'

'Of course. Everyone knows. We'll miss you.'

'I haven't said I'll take it yet.'

'But you will.' He smiled. 'Too good an opportunity to miss.'

'Yes.'

Yes, it was. So why did it now seem so unimportant? It was what she had worked for, had strived for.

She made a determined effort after that to be busy, concentrate, but every few minutes she would halt what she was doing and stare into space. How did you get over someone you didn't really know, shouldn't *get* to know? How did you stop yourself thinking about them? Wondering what they were doing? She'd never felt like this before. She was a sensible girl, she'd always been sensible... Perhaps that was the trouble, maybe if she'd embraced life the way Sheila did, she wouldn't be in this pickle now. And, yet, Sheila had wanted him to phone. He seemed to have that effect on all women.

The day seemed never-ending and, when she did get home, she saw to her astonishment that two sensor lights were positioned on the front of the flats. Tris's work? She wouldn't ask. She really would not ask, but she did hover, just for a moment, outside Eva's flat, before going determinedly into her own. Although, if she didn't ask, he might think she wasn't grateful. And she was. The residents, including herself, had always complained about the lack of light outside, but no one had ever done anything about it. It had taken a stranger—well, no, not a stranger exactly—but someone who didn't actually live here to rectify matters.

Before she could change her mind, she dropped her bag and walked quickly back to his flat and rapped on the door. If he hadn't opened it almost immediately, she might not have waited, but he did.

'Thank you for the lights,' she blurted. 'I won't stop. I just wanted to say thank you. Although I hope you didn't pay for them yourself. The residents could club together...'

He pulled her inside and closed the door. Squashed in the narrow hall, they stared at each other.

'I have done nothing today,' he said quietly. 'Everything I started, I stopped. Everywhere I went I forgot what I went for. I regret I sent you inside last night. And I want to kiss you. Make love to you. I want to hold you in my arms and be lost for minutes, hours, days.'

She said not a word. Couldn't. Didn't want to, just stared at him, her wide eyes fixed on his face.

'I kept thinking, we could have an affair. A brief, short, wonderful, affair. And then I would think, no, because I might want more. I should never have broken my leg. I should never have listened to Michael telling me about you. And I should have picked Michael up myself.' He took a deep breath, gave a quirky smile and said softly, 'Go away.'

She turned blindly to open the door and he halted

her. He put out his hand and then, as though unable to help himself, gently began to caress her shoulder through her thin jacket. 'No. Stay. Come and have a coffee. Talk to me—touch me. No,' he said quickly, 'don't, for God's sake, touch me.' Slumping against the wall, he gave the wryest of wry smiles. 'What are you doing to me, Kerith? What *are* you doing?'

'I don't know,' she whispered.

'But you feel the same?'

'Yes,' she agreed thickly.

Eyes still holding hers, he added, 'It would cause enormous complications: me in France; you in England; trying to find the time to meet; hasty; inadequate.'

'Yes.' And ultimate heartache, she thought.

She wanted to reach out, touch him, run her hands across his chest, his neck, wanted to be held, kissed, loved. But she must use her head. She must. And yet, if she did resist, wasn't it likely she would end up just as bitter and unsatisfied as her mother because she *hadn't* taken this step? But, to live in France, with no prospect of getting a job until she'd learned the language, dependent on Tris? She barely knew him.

'I've been standing here waiting for you to come home,' he confessed quirkily. 'Listening for the outer door to open, waiting for your footsteps. Now, is that foolish, or what?'

'Foolish,' she agreed as she continued to worry round the problem.

'And what have you been doing, Kerith Deaver?'

'Daydreaming,' she said softly. 'Sheila asked about you.'

'Who? Oh, yes, Sheila.'

'She hoped you might phone her. I was—jealous. Isn't that silly?'

'Crazy. How could I look at anyone else? So, what to do?'

'I don't know. We barely know each other.'

'No, and you don't want to feel like this, do you, Kerith?'

'Yes. No. I hate feeling like this and yet I want to, and I don't know what will happen or where it will end. You'll go back to France and forget me.'

'No.'

'No?' she asked hopefully.

'I shan't forget you. How could I? But I'm not husband material, Kerith, and I couldn't bear to hurt you.'

'Why aren't you?' she asked softly.

'Because of a dream, because of Michael, because of so many things. Why did you think me like your father?'

'Oh, because of the charm. He was charming.'

'And you didn't like him?'

'Yes. No. He left me,' she said stupidly. 'And he left me with a fear of rejection, a fear of being stranded without money, without a—home. I'm not a reckless sort of girl. If I had been,' she added quietly, 'would you have made love to me?'

'No.' His voice was thicker, gruffer, as he pulled her more warmly against him. 'I promised myself a long time ago that I wouldn't get emotionally involved again.' He gave a brief, husky laugh. 'And now look at me? I live in France, you live opposite my ex-sister-in-law and I can't, quite, see myself visiting you, making love to you, with her looking over my shoulder.'

'No.'

'And the reasons, the excuses, sound very spurious, don't they?'

'Yes.'

'Because we're both afraid of being hurt.'

She took a deep breath and wanted, very badly, to say that she would take a chance but, before she could do so, he continued, 'Because you've seen firsthand what can happen when the foundations between a couple aren't very secure, haven't you? And so have I,' he added softly. 'So, I can either go home tomorrow,' he resumed quietly, 'or I can stay until Eva returns at the end of the week.'

She should tell him to go. That would be safer. But she didn't want to. She wanted to know what it would be like to be made love to by—an expert.

'Stay,' she whispered and before the word was

completely out of her mouth he had drawn her into his arms and was kissing her.

Kissing him properly, thoroughly, was like nothing she had ever imagined, nothing she had ever dreamt of, and it went on for a very long time.

His arms were inside her jacket, hers were around his back, holding him, needing him. After the initial urgency, it slowed, became explorative, gentle. There was no heavy breathing, nor fumbling and, even in her hazy state of enjoyment, she was rather surprised and pleased. She did know how to respond, she found. With Tris, she knew.

He broke the kiss gently, lingeringly, and then threaded his hands through her thick hair. 'I've wanted to do that for a long time now. Ever since you smiled at me in your kitchen that first morning. I imagined how that full lower lip would look swollen from my kisses. And now I do know. It's very—arousing. You induce fantasies, Kerith,' he informed her softly, his eyes still on her mouth. 'And it's easy to be strong, insular, when you don't want anyone, don't fancy anyone... We'll go out,' he suddenly announced.

'Will we?' she asked in bewilderment.

He gave his quirky smile. 'Yes. It's safer. I'll take you out for a meal. Go and get ready. You have fifteen minutes.' He turned her, opened the door, and gently urged her out.

Feeling dazed, unreal, she walked slowly across

to her flat and into the bathroom. All she had ever read, heard, been told, about wanting someone, fancying someone, there had always seemed a sort of desperation about it. But she didn't feel desperate. He didn't seem to either. It was almost as though they had been waiting for this all their lives, knew there would be time.

Don't be silly, she told herself, and yet, that was how it felt. She did want to make love to him, but not in a scrabbling kind of way. She wanted it to be gentle and languorous and thorough.

A small frown on her face, she showered, then dressed in black trousers and shirt. She combed her hair, put on mascara and lipstick, collected her dark green jacket from the wardrobe and went to wait at the front door like an obedient child.

She wanted an affair with him. She could cope with that, couldn't she? When he came over to bring Michael, or pick him up, they could be together. She could take the new job, if she passed her exams; she would still have her security. So why did it sound and feel so unsatisfactory? From wanting nothing, she now wanted everything. And she couldn't, quite, let go of Eva's words that he had a short attention span and that once he'd conquered he lost interest, moved on. But he didn't look like a man who'd conquered. He looked like she felt. Dazed. Disbelieving. Thoughtful. If she'd been more experienced, knew more about men...

The doorbell rang and she jumped. She opened the door and he said simply, 'Come.'

And she did.

'I want you,' she said quietly a few minutes later. 'Am I allowed to say that?'

'Yes,' he agreed gently as they walked hand in hand along the High Street.

'I've spent so many years determinedly wrapping myself in my career that now I find I don't know how to behave.'

'You're doing fine,' he said quietly.

'Am I? I'm not a weak-willed person, Tris. I'm strong, capable, determined. I have a job I love, a job I'm very good at. I have my own flat, enough money to enjoy life, a small circle of friends. I *shape* my life.' Or she had.

'Because of your father,' he put in, 'because you don't want to ever rely on anyone but yourself.'

'Yes. And now, I feel—rudderless. Are you a Svengali figure who bends women to their will? Did you hypnotise me?'

He halted, stared down at her. 'I was just wondering the same thing. I don't even know where we're going.'

She looked at him, and started to laugh. 'How in God's name did you ever navigate your way round the world?'

'Luck?'

'I don't know you, do I?'

'No,' he agreed gently. 'Do you like Indian food?'

'Yes,' she agreed.

'Come on, then, there's an Indian restaurant over the road.'

They crossed over, were found a table in the window and, when they'd ordered, he asked quietly, 'Tell me about your father.'

'Why?' she asked curiously.

'Because he and your mother shaped you, made you what you are. He wasn't a good father or husband, was he?'

'No. Although I didn't know that when I was a child. I thought him perfect, a hero. Funny and kind. Loving. Much as Michael views you,' she said bravely, 'and that, I think, along with the things Eva said, was what made me believe you were like him.'

'Go on.'

And so she told him, as honestly as she could, about her father, her mother, about the sham of their marriage, and about the bitterness, about boyfriends not being allowed.

'You didn't rebel?'

'No,' she said. And that was weak-willed too, wasn't it?

'Because she made you feel guilty? To blame?'

'Yes. I thought he would come back. For years I thought that. *Knew* he would come. Because he loved me. But he never did. No cards on birthdays or at Christmas. No nothing. And now, there never will be,' she added sadly. 'I can't go and find him, ask him why he behaved as he did. I feel—incomplete.'

'And you're afraid that history might repeat itself? That you're unlovable?'

Thinking about it for a minute, she shook her head. 'I don't know. Not consciously, but maybe it's there at the back of my mind.'

'And you thought me like him? Because of Eva?'

'Only at first. Not later.'

'And if you hadn't known about me beforehand, if you took those things out of the equation, what's left, Kerith?'

'You,' she said simply. 'Charming, because you are. Amiable, and smiling; there's an amusement about you, a zest for life, and you watch me as though you too are puzzled by what's happening.'

'Yes, because I thought myself immune.'

'Because of your marriage?'

He hesitated a moment, then nodded.

Their wine was brought and whilst Tris poured it, she watched him. 'What was she like?' she asked curiously.

He looked at her, and then said gently, 'Ginny isn't for discussion.'

'But my father is? My life?'

'Yes.'

'That's hardly fair.'

'No. I'm not being fair, I know that, and I had no

intention of getting involved with you, much as I was attracted. For Michael's sake. For your sake, but I'm not like your father who sounds like a man who liked the easy options. No confrontations, no explanations, just go, start again, be nice, be charming, and hope no one will notice the weaknesses. I've had one failed marriage and, for Michael's sake, I won't risk another. I would never abandon him. Not for any reason.'

'I know that. You love him too much.'

'Yes, I do. He's my life, Kerith.'

Their meal arrived and they both leaned back to accommodate the dishes.

'And there's no room for anyone else?' she asked sadly.

'It isn't a question of room. Eat,' he prompted, and she picked up her fork and began on the meal, but she desperately wanted to know what it was a question of.

'I laughed, that first time we met,' he said quietly. 'After you'd delivered your opinion of the puce shirt, I laughed. I wanted to see you again, know what you were like, but I think I knew, even then, that it would be dangerous and I promised myself that I would steer clear of you. Circumstances decreed otherwise.'

'Yes.'

'And even then I could have walked away. I didn't want to. And that was selfish.'

'Sometimes,' she began slowly, cautiously, 'things happen.'

'Yes,' he agreed quickly. 'Do people who don't know you think you arrogant and conceited?' he asked unexpectedly.

She choked on a mouthful of food and he hastily handed her a glass of water. 'How do *I* know what people think?' she demanded when she could finally speak.

'Because men always assume that women do. Not many men ask you out, do they?'

Wondering where on earth all this was leading, she shook her head.

'Because they're afraid of rejection.'

'No, because I put them off with my stuffy manner.'

'No, your stuffy manner, as you put it, would be a challenge,' he argued. 'But they would also assume that because you are so beautiful your diary would be full to bursting point. And so they don't ask.'

'That's ridiculous.' Although *women* seemed to think she had a full social life. Hundreds of boyfriends.

'No, it isn't,' he denied.

'It didn't seem to affect you!' she said somewhat tartly.

'No, but then, my invitations have always been to

thank you for something, haven't they? And you aren't in the least conceited.'

'Arrogant?' she asked.

He merely smiled. 'When we went to that restaurant in France and everyone looked at you, you were embarrassed. And when we came in here, and the same thing happened, you looked quickly away. And, I've also noticed, on the few occasions I've been with you, that you never make eye contact with men.'

'No, because they seem to take it as an open invitation.'

'But you did make eye contact with me,' he said with a small smile, 'because you were angry and defiant and almost dared me to even *think* of liking you.'

'Because you unnerved me. I told you, I don't know much about men. I don't know how to flirt, tease. I don't know what to say when they pay me compliments.'

'Thank you, is what you say.' He smiled. 'Are you like your mother?'

'Like her?' she echoed as she thought about it, then shook her head. 'No, but then, I didn't have her life.'

'What did she do when your father left?'

'Got a job. We had no money; he left nothing. She worked on the checkout at a supermarket.'

'And became even more bitter?'

'Yes.'

'And if it happened to you, what would you do?'

About to give him a flip answer, she paused, thought about it, and then said quietly, and really rather determinedly, 'Get a life.'

'Yes, and so you see, you can't equate what happened to your mother to what might happen to you.'

'But their lives *shaped* mine.'

'Of course they did, as my life has shaped me and that of my son. We all have to make our own mistakes and learn from them.'

'Which is why you won't remarry? Because of your mistakes?'

'Maybe.'

'And Eva?' she probed, wanting to know more. 'You always speak of her with a sort of wry amusement. Why?'

He shrugged. 'A defence mechanism against her anger, I expect.'

'And Michael? Does he ever ask why you and she don't get on? Because you don't, do you?'

'No, and yes. He has asked. Once. I told him that it was a personality clash, the way he doesn't like some boy at school. I don't hate her, he knows that.'

'And his mother?'

'I answer anything he wants to know. Take him to her grave so that he can lay flowers.'

'Does he know you were separated before she died?'

'Yes.'

'And did he want to know why?'

'Of course,' he answered patiently. 'I don't go into details, just tell him that we found we no longer loved each other.'

'But she did love him?'

'Yes. No more questions.' He idly forked his food around on his plate as though he were no longer hungry, and then continued quietly, musingly, 'You make me dream, Kerith. I push the dreams away and back they come. Like slow waves on the shore, lapping, lapping, gradually eating away at the sand. You're such a contradiction. Shy, abrupt, impatient, and yet there's an air of slow langour about you that keeps drawing me in, wanting more. You don't, at first glance, look like a kind, thoughtful person, but you are. Kind to Michael, Mrs Davies... Sheila said you were nice.' He gave a small smile. 'She followed me to lunch and so I used the occasion to ask about you. Discreetly, of course.

'She said that when you first joined the firm, everyone expected you to be snooty, arrogant, and you weren't. Everyone liked you, she said. That you help people out.'

Embarrassed, she looked down. 'Be a sad old world,' she murmured, 'if you couldn't help people out now and again.'

'Yes, but it isn't any of that, or not entirely. I don't know what it is about you that attracts me so.

It's not your beauty because, if you weren't a nice person inside, your beauty wouldn't attract. I'm not explaining this very well…' He gave an awkward smile. 'I don't want to dance on moonbeams, Kerith, I want to draw you into a warm cave and keep you there, safe, and mine. I want everything to be— slow.'

Much as she felt. Extraordinarily, much as she felt.

'And it wouldn't be fair to you.'

'Who's to say what's fair?' she asked quickly.

'I am. You have an exciting new job to look forward to and although I would, more than anything, like to get to know you…' he gave a deep sigh '…I'm not a hasty man, Kerith. Now,' he added with a small frown. Leaning back, he pushed his plate to one side. 'I didn't think I was like this,' he murmured in self-disgust. 'I'm really quite astonished at myself.'

'Will you ring me when you return to France?' she asked hopefully.

'No. It would be best not.'

'That isn't what I was asking. I don't want it to end here. Perhaps we could meet from time to time.' She could juggle it, her job and him. Of course she could. Other people did. But she couldn't let him go. Not like this. 'Not here, if you don't want,' she added without looking at him, 'but…'

'Clandestinely?'

She grimaced. 'Sounds awful, doesn't it? But if you don't want Eva or Michael to know... Don't make me beg,' she whispered.

He took her hands across the table. 'I don't want you hurt. Come on, let's get out of here. You can make the coffee.'

She tried for lightness to mask her pain. 'Gee, thanks.'

'That's it, keep it light, Kerith, I'm a very fragile man.'

She felt pretty fragile herself.

CHAPTER SIX

THE next few days went surprisingly fast. Too fast. And, on the question of an affair, they would wait and see, he said. Get to know each other better first.

'We know each other better,' Kerith argued.

'Not better enough.'

'Was your marriage hasty?' she asked, guessing.

'Yes.'

'Oh. Am I like her?'

'No.'

'Then…'

'No!' he said firmly. 'Dear God, Kerith, don't make it harder. I want you with every fibre of my being, you know that, but I can't and won't put you in a position where you might get hurt.'

'Might,' she said quickly latching onto what she saw as a weakness. 'I might *not* get hurt.'

'But there's every probability that you will,' he said simply, defeatedly almost.

'But *why*?'

'Because it was my fault the marriage went wrong. I haven't changed. I'm not a different person, and if Michael weren't involved I wouldn't hesitate to have an affair with you.'

'But not marriage?'

'No,' he said adamantly.

That was all he would say on the subject, despite her constant pleading, and so they went out every evening in order to get to know each other better, and because it was safer. And, until their last evening together, they said their goodnights in the corridor.

They did silly things, light-hearted things, or tried very hard to be light-hearted, went up to Trafalgar Square on the bus. She hadn't been on a bus in years. Didn't even know where they *went*. They wandered hand in hand through Soho, Leicester Square; watched the crowds, ate wherever they fancied. The next night they found a local jazz club. She hadn't even known it existed. Nor that he liked jazz. There was a small dance floor and, despite his gangling appearance, he was a very good dancer.

He was also clever, had an extraordinary knowledge on a great range of subjects, and so they talked, and kissed, but they didn't make love. Frustration was her constant companion.

'Do we know each other better yet?' she would ask each night, and he would give a shaky smile and say, 'No.'

It was a hard, aching, time, both aware of time ticking away and on the Friday evening, the last evening they would have together before he went back to France, they stood in her lounge and held each other close.

She found it hard, now, to imagine a life without him. Held in his arms, her head tucked beneath his chin, aware of the warmth of him, the length, his arousal and her own, she gently stroked her hands down his long back. She had a need to keep touching him. His hand, his face, to smile at him, to have him smile in return.

'I shall remember the smell of your hair, the feel of you against me... This is absurd, Kerith.'

'I know,' she whispered, 'there's a nice big bed a few yards away.'

'No. I have to go soon.'

She looked up at him in despair. 'Then, we'll meet, won't we? *Won't* we?' she persisted.

'Clandestinely?'

'Yes.' She searched his face, no longer a fool's face, and she wondered, now, how she had ever thought it was. Raising one hand, she touched her fingers to his cheek, his jaw, as though she would need to remember the feel of him.

'I'll ring you,' he promised.

Well, it was a start. 'When?'

'Monday evening.'

'Thank you. It's not very flattering, you know, to have to beg.'

'I know. You think it isn't tearing me apart too?'

'I don't know. If it was, you'd tell me properly. Is it because of Michael? Because Ginny doesn't come out of this very well and you'd be afraid I'd tell him?'

He put his fingers over her mouth.

She removed his hand and held it in her own. 'I want you,' she said simply as she stared into his blue eyes. Eyes that looked trustworthy, honest, and he groaned, crushed her against him and, for the first time ever, he kissed her with a sort of desperation. The fullness of his arousal pressed against her. His long fingers shook as they dealt with the buttons on her shirt before trailing them slowly, agonisingly, to the full swell of her breasts. His mouth followed, teasing, seductive and she closed her eyes. It was the most beautiful feeling in the world being touched by the man she—loved. Opening her eyes, she stared at his bent head, slowly ran her fingers through his crisp hair. Loved. They were both shaking.

His eyes looked too bright as he raised his head, his breathing heavy and slow, as was hers. They looked at each other for a very, very, long time. 'I have one or two things to do before I go to pick up Michael,' he said thickly. 'I told Lena I would be there by nine. I have a cab booked.'

She glanced at the clock, saw that it was just gone eight, and nodded.

'Don't look at me like that. All eyes and— Don't see me out.' He released her and turned abruptly away to stand at the window.

She knew why.

Her eyes on his back, she swallowed, licked dry lips before attempting to speak. 'Will you leave me your address and telephone number?'

He hesitated and she thought he was going to refuse, but then he nodded and she gave a breath of relief.

She fetched pad and pen and handed them to him. Without touching. He quickly scribbled them down and handed the pad back.

She looked at it, then smiled, gave a small, husky, laugh. 'The Tram House?'

He turned and gave a strained smile of his own. 'When I first arrived in the village they had trouble with my name and so I spoke slowly, as one does, and they thought my name was Tris Tram. Monsieur Tram, and so my home was referred to as Maison Tram. Claude, the builder, thought it very amusing to burn the words into a piece of wood and hang it over the front door. And because he is learning English, and because I *am* English and sometimes have English visitors, he called it The Tram House. The Tram House it has remained. It now has a very superior sign made by the local blacksmith as a house-warming present.'

Unable to look at him for too long without wanting to touch him, she put the pad back on the bureau and asked, 'They like you there, don't they? Michael said how everyone was very friendly.'

'I hope they like me. Certainly I like them.'

'Why France?'

'Accident, impulse. I had no burning desire to be a Francophile, had never even thought of living in France until I was driving back that way from Spain. I saw the house, a derelict ruin, and I fell in love with it. It seemed such a shame to let it fall down. All that once beautiful architecture lost. I don't think I was intending to live in it, just restore it and sell it. The villagers thought I was to be their new neighbour. They made me welcome, looked after me, took Michael to their hearts and so I didn't have the nerve to suggest I wasn't going to live there. And now, I can't imagine living anywhere else. It's almost feudal in a way. They look after their own, help each other out, and I rather like that.'

'Sounds nice.'

'It is. Goodbye, Kerith.'

'*Not* goodbye,' she said fiercely.

'No.'

She heard the front door close softly behind him. It couldn't end like this. She wouldn't let it. But why, why, was he fighting this war with himself? Whatever had happened with Ginny, he surely couldn't think this would be the same.

Biting her lip, she turned away, trailed her hand where he had touched. Perhaps she would see it one day, his house in France. Perhaps she would live there. She wanted to chase after him, tell him, ask him... But he would ring. On Monday. And they would meet. And they would make love. Spend the night together. She could get up early from wherever they were, drive to work the next morning.

Still turning she came face to face with herself in the mirror over the mantelpiece. She looked flushed, her mouth swollen, her hair in disarray. Her eyes looked sleepy, heavy.

Her shirt was still unbuttoned, the swell of her breasts clearly visible above the black lace of her bra. He'd tugged down the cup, set his mouth to one nipple... With a little shudder, she turned away. And if they had made love? Committed to each other? Told the world? What would Eva have said? Not that it *mattered* what Eva said. But Michael? And then, if it all ended, as it might, what then?

He would ring her, wouldn't he? Yes, he'd said he would. And they would meet. In a hotel room somewhere. For months, years, to come? Until Michael was grown?

Or would she go out to France, live with him there? If he ever asked her. She could learn the language, find a job. Other people managed it. Dad's live-in girlfriend, Michael would say, or, this is my stepmother. She had some savings, she wouldn't *have* to live off him. And, if it didn't work out, she could come back; she was fully trained, could always get a job.

She worried too much, she decided. Analysed too much. Everything would be all right.

Hard to remember that she'd known him such a short time. And once she saw him in his own environment maybe, talked to people who knew him...

She gave an impatient little shake of her head—and saw his wallet sitting on the side table. Picking it up, she ran her fingers over the soft leather. He would need it. Glancing at the clock, she saw that only ten minutes had passed. He'd said he had one or two things to do in the flat... One last time.

Hurrying out, leaving her door open, she quickly tapped on his, then gave a little groan as she saw that her blouse was still unbuttoned. An open invitation. She began trying to do it up one-handed as he opened the door.

She looked up—and flew into his arms. 'You *will* ring?'

'Yes,' he agreed thickly.

Moving back a little, she looked at him again. He really was rather special. Endearing. His hair was rumpled, and his eyes looked as sleepy as her own.

'You left your wallet,' she explained as she handed it over.

He took it, shoved it into his back pocket, then reached out to touch her, thread his fingers through her hair. 'One last kiss?' he asked, and his voice was throaty, sexy.

Their mouths were a centimetre apart when the

angry voice intruded and they leapt apart almost guiltily. Or she did. She wasn't so sure about Tris.

'My God!' Eva exclaimed. 'It didn't take you long, did it?'

'Hello, Eva,' he drawled. His voice sounded strained.

'Don't hello me, you bastard. And what the hell are you doing in my flat? I didn't give you permission to stay here.'

'No,' he agreed.

Dropping her case, she turned her angry gaze on Kerith, stared pointedly at her undone blouse. 'You fool,' she spat. 'I told you what he was like. Did you listen? No. And if you've run up a massive phone bill...' she turned angrily on Tris to accuse '...talking to your legion of women...'

'I haven't,' he denied.

Kerith stared from one to the other. She had known that Eva didn't like him, but to be so venomous...

'Yes, you do well to look bewildered,' she taunted. 'I *told* you what he was like! He walked *out* on her when Michael was a few months old. He walked *out*! Didn't you?' she said gratingly at Tris.

'Yes,' he agreed.

'She could have *starved* for all you cared. She *loved* you.'

He didn't answer, merely leaned against the doorframe and crossed his arms over his chest.

Kerith felt numb. She didn't want to know this. She really didn't. And why wasn't he *angry* at being spoken to like this? Why wasn't he defending himself?

'They had a nice house in Putney, a nice life,' Eva continued, 'or so I thought. And then he left. Just walked out.' Her eyes still on Tris, defiant, angry, she spoke to Kerith as though he were deaf or blind or dumb. 'He was an architect, a good one, clever... Boy, was he clever. He has degrees I've never even heard of. Clever, manipulative and selfish. He didn't only walk out on Ginny, but on his partner. Left him to deal with all the ongoing clients, everything. As he left my sister. She was *devastated*.'

'It's nothing to do with me,' Kerith whispered.

'No, it isn't,' she agreed coldly. 'And for goodness sake do up your shirt! You look like a...'

'Enough,' Tris put in and his voice now was cold. 'Berate me if you must but you leave Kerith out of it.'

'Like you did?' she scoffed. 'What is it with you?' she demanded. 'The thrill of the chase? The need to overcome someone's reluctance? Like Kerith's? Because she *was* reluctant, I know she was. You're like her father.'

Startled, Kerith stared at her. 'How do you know about my father?'

She gave an irritable shrug. 'Your mother. When

she came up one day and you weren't home. I invited her into the flat to wait for you. She told me about him.'

'Commiserated, did you?' Tris drawled.

'Yes!' she spat the word out. 'Just because you have money you think you can walk all over everyone, that ordinary, little, people don't *matter*! Well, they do! And if you try to stop me seeing my nephew...'

'I have no intention of stopping you.'

'You'd better not. *I'm* not like Ginny. I *fight*!'

'I know.'

She stared at him, her throat working, her hands bunched at her sides, and her voice shook as she continued her tirade. 'And how's Suzanne? Or is she history?'

'History,' he agreed.

'Poor girl.' Bitterness in every line of her, she turned to Kerith. 'He invited her to live with him in his house. She gave up her life, her home—and now, it seems, he's thrown her out. Compensate her did you?'

'No.'

'No,' she agreed. 'Why should you? Women are to be used, aren't they?'

'Greek romance not work out, then?'

She went to hit him and he lazily blocked her hand.

'Sorry,' he apologised mockingly, 'cheap shot.'

She flushed and her mouth tightened in anger. 'At least I stick to one at a time. Neither do I have responsibilities. I feel sorry for that boy...'

His voice hardened. 'Then, don't.'

'Growing up in an environment where an army of women can march through his home,' she continued as though he hadn't spoken. 'How many other Suzannes have there been?'

'Oh, one or two.'

'See?' She turned to Kerith to ask.

Kerith stared at Tris, her eyes anxious. He stared right back.

'I don't believe he's like you say...' she began, only to be shot down by Eva.

'Then, you're a fool! Did he ask you to go back to France with him?'

'No,' she whispered.

'Meet you somewhere?'

'No.' Because he hadn't. She'd been the one to suggest that. Feeling sick and wretched, she continued to stare at Tris. His gaze was mocking. Not contrite, embarrassed, but mocking.

'Is it true?' Kerith whispered.

'What do you think?' he asked.

'I don't know,' she said helplessly.

'Of course you know!' Eva snapped. 'You just don't want to admit it!'

First impressions were the right impressions. Someone had said that to her once, and it was true.

More often than not, it was true. She had known what he was like when she'd first met him. But he wasn't. He *wasn't*! He would never have given her his address if he had been.

Feeling sick, almost ashamed, eyes still fixed on Tris, she asked tremulously, 'You aren't going to deny anything?'

'No.'

'You did walk out on your wife?'

'Yes,' he agreed, still mocking, still staring at her with that hateful derision.

'And you took Michael with you?'

'Yes.'

'Yes!' Eva cut in viciously. 'And left her heart-broken. He took her *baby*, Kerith!'

'There must have been a reason...' she began.

'Of course there was a reason! The man's a rat! Aren't you?' she asked him.

He didn't answer, and so Eva continued as though she couldn't stop, as though she had gone too far now to back down. 'It's probably why you went to live in France! No one in England would speak to you! And maybe the laws on child abduction are different in France. Whatever the reasons, she couldn't get him back, could she? And *that's* what contributed to her death!' she finished bitterly.

'No.'

'Yes! You didn't see how crazy she was, manic almost, she *died* because of you! Now get out of my flat! I don't *ever* want to see you again! And leave Kerith alone!'

He glanced at her. 'You want to be left alone, Kerith?'

She stood mute.

He gave a mocking smile and turned into the flat to collect his belongings.

Eva glared after him, one arm wrapped almost comfortingly against her sore ribs. She gave one last look at Kerith, grabbed up her case, marched in behind him and closed the door.

Left alone in the corridor, Kerith stared blindly at the polished wood. It wasn't true, she told herself, he wasn't like that. There was a reason for him leaving his wife and taking the baby, there *had* to be.

Turning, she walked slowly back to her flat. Eva had deliberately brought up that Tris was like her father because she'd *known* what her father was like. And she'd said all those things because she hadn't wanted Kerith to like Tris. Why? And now that she'd seen they were together, was even more determined to break them up. Why? And why would she lie? Although, he hadn't denied anything, had he? Hadn't argued or become angry. Even if Eva told the truth, why hadn't he been angry? Cared? Because Kerith really *wasn't* important enough? Because he didn't *care* what she believed? Or... Slamming her hand angrily against the wall, she stalked into the lounge. Perhaps he'd thought she would defend him. Automatically know none of it was true. And Suzanne had probably been his housekeeper, or something. She closed her eyes tight, willed the pain to go away.

But if it *was* all true, was that why Tris said he would never remarry? Because he'd been a lousy husband? Had driven his wife to her death? No, she couldn't believe that.

Maybe Eva exaggerated. She *was* very bitter... Don't, she told herself. Don't make excuses. You knew what he was like. You always knew. But she didn't. She *didn't*.

And he'd known, hadn't he? As soon as he'd heard Eva's voice, he'd known what would happen. Because it had happened before? And *that* was why he didn't want a relationship with her? Because he had known what would happen? Knew that, at some point or another, Eva would tell her about him?

And she needed to know the truth. Now.

Running back to the hall, she dragged open the front door and was just in time to see Tris push through the end door. She hurried after him and caught him up at the bottom.

'Tris!' she called breathlessly.

He didn't even pause, just pushed open the outer door and stepped through. She grabbed his arm. 'Tris!' she said urgently. 'We have to talk.'

He unpeeled her hand from his arm and, without looking at her, said, 'We have nothing to talk about.'

'Yes, we do!'

He turned, stared at her as though he'd never seen her before, and then he walked away. With perfect timing, a cab drew up at the kerb, and he climbed in.

'No,' she whispered to herself. 'No.' It couldn't end like this. It couldn't.

Eva was waiting for her when she walked back inside. 'I told you what he was like,' she said tremulously.

Kerith ignored her, walked past towards her own flat.

'I *told* you!' she shouted. She grabbed Kerith's arm, and halted her. 'Don't let him hurt you!' she pleaded. 'Not like Ginny. I *like* you!'

'Oh, Eva!' she exclaimed helplessly. 'You can't live my life for me, you *can't*!'

'I'm not trying to, but don't you see? He isn't *right* for you!'

'Yes, he is. I'm sorry, but he is.'

'Then, you're a fool!' she almost yelled. 'A stupid, blind fool! You're clutching at straws. Just like Ginny did. Are you really so arrogant that you think you'll be the one to hold him, just because you're *pretty*? Ginny was pretty! He's like your father! He *is*. As soon as your mother told me about him I *knew* he was like Tris.'

'No. Please don't say any more.' Hurrying into

her flat, she shut the door. He wasn't like Eva said. He wasn't.

She spent the whole weekend thinking about it. Every minute of every day. She went over and over it a hundred million times. Saw his face, heard his voice. He'd *expected* her to believe Eva. Expected her to be angry, accusing, to walk away.

There were two sides to every story. Eva only had her sister's. There had to be a reason, a very good reason, why Tris had walked out on Ginny. Had to be a very good reason for him to take the baby.

On the Monday, she went through work like an automaton and, when evening came, when it got nearer and nearer to the time when Tris would have phoned, she sat in the chair, in the dark, and stared at the instrument. He wouldn't phone now. Of course he wouldn't.

He might.

No. And suddenly, career, independence, didn't matter a damn. Tris mattered. Only Tris.

She could ring him, ask him, but he wouldn't tell her, would he? Why? Pride? Honour?

The affairs didn't matter—or, not much—it was usual for a single man to have affairs. She doubted he flaunted them in front of his son. *Knew* he didn't. That she could believe of him, but his marriage? Had Ginny found out about an affair and told him to go? So why had he taken the baby? And why hadn't Ginny fought to get the baby back?

It didn't really make sense.

And it wasn't only Eva, was it? He didn't get on with the grandmother either, did he? Although, she only had Eva's word for that, certainly he'd never said anything about it. He hadn't said very much about anything. The only thing she did know with any certainty was that he loved his son.

And that she loved him.

She hated indecision, hated not knowing and she could not, would not, spend the rest of her life wondering. And so she would go out, she decided. Talk to him, because it wasn't going to go away, she knew that. His face would stay in her mind. His blue eyes, his quirky smile. The way he had kissed her.

Right, no more vacillating. She would go out. To France. She had time off due to her, maybe she could take it next week. It was the only way she was going to get it out of her head.

Get him out.

Or draw him back in.

CHAPTER SEVEN

'KERITH!' Max exploded angrily. 'You can't take next week off! I have goodness knows how much stuff coming in to be catalogued.'

'Oh, yes, sorry, I forgot.'

'Not like you. What's wrong?'

'Nothing I just need to sort out something personal.'

'Then, take the rest of the week off. Yes?'

'Yes, thank you.'

'Then, go and do it. I like my staff efficient, and I have to tell you that these last few weeks I've come very close to giving you a severe reprimand. And yesterday, well, yesterday doesn't even bear thinking about. This isn't *like* you!'

'No,' she agreed.

'Go on, get out of here,' he said gruffly. 'Leave your desk, Sheila can sort it out. About time she did something to earn her keep!'

Knowing it for the lie it was because Sheila worked as hard as anyone, as he well knew, she gave him a small smile. 'Thanks, Max.'

She told Sheila she would be away for the week, and then drove home. With luck she'd be able to get a cabin on the overnight ferry from Portsmouth.

She rang the ferry company, packed enough for a few days, found her French map, her passport, even some francs she had left over from her holiday, had some lunch and, even though it was far too early, she drove down to Portsmouth. She wanted to be away. Needed to be doing something.

She arrived in France at eight the next morning. *Déjà vu*. Almost the same route she had taken in July. Rennes, Nantes, Cholet, and all the time she rehearsed in her mind what she was going to say, ask. She stopped for lunch at midday and then drove on towards Parthenay.

As she neared the medieval town she had to stop several times to ask the way and then, finally, she arrived at the small village where Tris lived. Grey stone houses, a twisting main street, a pretty church. Beginning to worry because she was getting to the edge of the village and hadn't seen the house yet, she slowed, tried to remember all that Michael had told her, and then she saw it.

It stood back from the road a little way and she parked beside the battered old truck and a dusty car. There was no one around that she could see and so she looked at the house. It was beautiful. Half-timbered, large, rather quaint in a way. The garden wasn't. It looked like a builder's yard, piles of sand, gravel, a cement mixer. An old barn to one side was covered in scaffolding.

And she was nervous, she found. Supposing he didn't want her here? Suppose all that Eva had said was true? No, she denied to herself. It wasn't. She would stake her life on that. Eva had been wrong.

She took a deep breath for courage, got out, picked up her bag, because she never went anywhere without it, and quietly closed the door behind her.

She carefully picked her way across the rubble and, because her nerves were stretched so tight, when someone spoke from behind her, she jumped in fright.

'Mademoiselle?'

Turning, she stared at a short, tubby, man wearing a battered hat. *'Bonjour,'* she began, and he smiled.

'You are English. I have the speaking of it,' he stated proudly.

'Yes. Are you Claude?'

'But, of course.' He beamed. 'You know of me?'

'Yes, from Michael. I'm Kerith Deaver.'

He looked utterly delighted and thrust out his hand to be shaken. 'Kerith I know. Michael speaks of you. The pretty one, he says, and so you are.'

'Thank you. Is Tris here? I need to see him about something.'

He looked worried. 'Does he not know you are coming?'

'No.'

'He does not like...' He went to scratch his head,

encountered the hat, and snatched it off. 'My apologies.'

'That's all right,' she murmured automatically. 'I just need to ask him something.'

Indecision pulling at his round face, he suddenly made up his mind. 'He is out back. Take the path through the 'edge.'

'Thank you.' With a last, rather lame, smile, she headed carefully in the direction he'd indicated. He does not like—visitors? Is that what Claude had been going to say?

Once free of the rubble, she walked more easily along the unmade up path. There was a small gap in the ''edge' as he'd called it, and she pushed through and halted. She could see for miles. A small village in the distance, a church spire, fields, a lake, or river. To her left were several horses in a field, and to her right, a small wooden seat tucked against the hedge where Tris sat, his long jean-clad legs thrust out before him. Her heart lurched at the sight of him and she had to bite back the little gasp that formed in her throat. She was in love with this man. And whatever he was, whatever he had done, wasn't going to make the blindest bit of difference to that love.

She had known how she felt but she hadn't *comprehended* how it would feel to lose him. She knew now.

There was a reason for all that had happened. A

very good reason. She didn't know if he loved her, didn't know if anything would come of her visit. But he had been attracted to her. It was a start. Something to build on.

He looked sad, she thought. Lonely. His dark blue work shirt was crumpled, his thick boots encased in mud. He held a mug in his hand and as she watched he suddenly and what looked like angrily tossed the dregs of whatever he had been drinking onto the rough grass and got abruptly to his feet.

He turned, saw her, and froze.

So did she. Held her breath in her body and quietly examined his face.

'Hello, Tris.' She had no idea how anxious her expression was, how wide her eyes.

'What are you doing here?' It sounded as though it had been an effort for him to speak, and she took comfort from that.

'I needed to talk to you.'

'We have nothing to say to each other.'

'Yes, we do. I don't want to know about the affairs, the other women, because they're none of my business; they all happened before we met. But I do need to know about Ginny.'

He gave a mirthless smile. 'You know about Ginny.'

'No, I know what Eva said about her. Please, tell me.'

'It's not for discussion.'

'It is if we're to be married.'

His look was of incredulity, and then he gave a bark of very unamused laughter. 'Who said anything about marriage?'

'I did. I love you.'

'Then, you're a fool. Goodbye, Kerith.' He gave her one last look of derision and walked past her.

You're lying, she thought. You want me as much as I want you. She wasn't very experienced, didn't know much about men, but that first look, when he'd first seen her, had been—anguished.

Turning, she hurried after him. No one had said it would be easy. What had she expected, that he would fall into her arms? Beg her forgiveness?

She followed him into the house through a side door, didn't really notice any details, just kept her eyes fixed on his long back. He halted at the wide French doors that looked over the rear, and very tangled, garden.

'Still here?' he asked without turning.

'Yes. Tell me.'

'There's nothing to tell. Michael will be home soon and I want you gone.'

'We were going to meet, make love.'

'Have sex,' he corrected coarsely. 'Don't romanticise it. We would have met, had sex,' he mocked harshly, 'and it might have lasted a few weeks, months, and then I would have ended it. An interlude. I'm sure it would have been very nice, but...'

'But you weren't falling in love with me,' she stated.

'No. I don't fall in love. I have affairs.'

'I don't believe you.'

She couldn't see his expression, but she suspected it was flat, distant. His shoulders were tense, his back stiff.

'Believe it,' he said. 'I probably wouldn't even have rung you.'

'Yes, you would.'

'Kerith...'

'No, please listen. Whatever happened between you and your wife, Eva only knows one side of it. She doesn't know the truth. Does she?'

'Of course she knows the truth.'

That halted her, just for a moment, but then she realised that, yes, Eva could know the truth, a different truth. Feeling her way through it, groping in the dark really, she continued, 'It's happened before, hasn't it? As soon as you heard Eva's voice, you knew what was about to occur. I was supposed to be shocked, hurt, disenchanted. But I was numb. And, afterwards, I thought about it and thought about it. It doesn't make sense, Tris.'

'Everything she said was true.'

'The facts, yes,' she agreed. 'But now I need the reasons. Please tell me what really happened.'

'No.'

'Which means that something did,' she said

softly. She walked up behind him and put her hand on his back. He went rigid. And then, with an inarticulate little cry, he threw his mug on the floor, where it shattered, and turned to haul her into his arms.

'There, that wasn't so hard, was it?' she asked. Her voice was shaking.

His words muffled by her shoulder, he demanded, 'Don't you *ever* take rejection?'

'No.' Not this time.

He took a deep breath and lifted his head. 'You're insane.'

'I'm in love.'

'Are you?' His hands fisted in her hair, he stared down into her beautiful face. 'I'm glad you came,' he said thickly. The look on his face said that it mattered very much that she had. 'But it won't work.'

'It can,' she pleaded.

'No.'

She didn't believe him. *Couldn't* believe him. It mattered too much. 'You wouldn't have come to me?'

'No.'

'Because?'

'Because I can't tell you,' he said thickly before he kissed her. A long, lingering, urgent, kiss. He held her tight against him and let out a long breath. 'Marriage?' he asked shakily.

'It just came out,' she said anxiously excusing herself. 'It's what I want, but... Why can't you tell me? Because she's dead? Because you still love her?'

'No.'

'Because of Michael? I won't tell him,' she promised. The same arguments, the same things she'd asked before and before and before. 'I know you said you would never remarry, but you did say we could have a relationship.'

'*You* said,' he pointed out gently as he smoothed her face, her hair, as though he couldn't help himself. 'But if we did, you would always wonder. It would eat away at you bit by bit. Why? Why did he leave her? Why did he take her child?'

He was right, she knew he was. It *would* eat away at her, but there was a reason for all that had happened. She knew there was, and it wasn't to his detriment.

'You don't know me, Kerith.'

'No,' she agreed as she stared worriedly up at him. 'But I do know what you aren't. How many times have you been...caught with a woman before?'

'By Eva? Never.'

'Never?' she asked in astonishment.

'No, she never knew the others.'

Just tortured herself that there *were* others? she wondered.

'Not that there were very many,' he added. 'Just, female company, from time to time.'

'And you weren't in love with them?'

'No.'

'With me?'

He stared deep into her eyes, searched them, and then nodded. 'Yes, I'm in love with you. From liking, being amused by you, I ended up loving.'

'Then, why walk away from *me*?'

'Because I couldn't bear to see your face, because it was a very much needed reminder that I shouldn't have become involved with you, and because all that she said was true, I was a lousy husband. I should never have stayed at Eva's apartment, I knew that. It was selfish and stupid, because I knew how furious she would be if she ever found out. I always knew how it would end.'

'Which is why you wouldn't make love to me.'

'Yes.'

'But you can now, can't you?' Stroking her hands up and down his chest, she whispered, 'I don't want to spend the rest of my life not knowing how it would be. Imagining, wanting.'

He took a deep breath, then let it all out. He moved his thumbs to her lower lip and watched himself touch it, stroke it. 'I'd locked you away in my mind, forced away the pain... Dear God, Kerith, I want you so.'

'Then, have me,' she said simply.

His eyes still on her mouth, he cautioned, 'She will say things.'

'Eva?'

'Yes.'

'I'm a big girl.'

He gave a small, sad smile. 'Yes, you are, aren't you? I want to protect you.'

'We can't protect from *every* eventuality, can we?'

'No,' he agreed and lifted his eyes to hers. 'I married in haste once.'

'We don't have to get married.'

'Yes, we do, because I don't want anything less.'

'Neither do I.'

'You're a very determined lady.'

'Bossy,' she agreed as her heart began to beat just that little bit faster. 'I like to shape my own destiny. I don't like other people doing it for me. Not Eva. Not Ginny. Kiss me again.'

He gave a shaky laugh. 'Do your own kissing.'

Which she never had, she realised. Cautious herself, she had always let him be the instigator. A smile in her eyes as she looked up at him, she murmured, 'I came late to love, I'm a little inexperienced.'

'Ah, don't,' he groaned, 'this is killing me.' His hands against her back, rubbing, gentling, he began to rain kisses over her upturned face: her brow, her nose, her mouth. They were urgent and draining, and then he forced himself away. 'We only have half an hour before Michael comes home from school.'

'And half an hour is a great deal better than a lifetime of nothing. Dear God, Tris, my body *aches*.'

He scooped her up, prompting a little yell of surprise, and carried her out of the room and up an ornate wooden staircase. She reached up to brush the thick hair off his forehead. 'I love you,' she whispered. 'I've never been able to imagine saying that to someone. Never, somehow, expected it to happen. And now, I'm all of a dither.'

'So am I.' He carried her into his room and laid her on his wide bed where he stood looking down at her for long, long moments. 'I've dreamt about this. Imagined you here, in my house. I didn't think it would ever happen. I love you, and I want it to be special and lingering. I don't want to have to hastily scramble into my clothes because Michael is coming. I'm aroused, and aching, and...'

'We can wait. Can't we? Tonight, when he's in bed. Something to savour. Something to look forward to.'

He sat on the edge of the bed and reached out to touch her face. His hand was hot. Almost burning. He trailed his fingers to her throat, stopped, and gave a wry, rather shaky, smile. 'I daren't go any further. I've never felt like this in my life.'

'Not even with Ginny?'

His face clouded. 'No. It wasn't like this.'

'Tell me,' she pleaded. 'I know you don't want to, but if you could just tell me *some* of it.'

'Like why I left her and took the baby? Because he was mine,' he said simply.

'But what about Ginny?'

'She didn't want him.'

'She didn't try to get him *back*?'

'No. Shocked?' he asked. 'Of course you are. So was I. I was twenty-eight when we married, and she was nineteen, pretty and appealing. I'd done all my growing up, or thought I had. I was a bit of an idealist, I think—and I thought I was in love. It was a crazy, stupid, hasty marriage in the face of her mother's disapproval. Her father had died years before and Lena brought the girls up alone. She thought Ginny too young. She was right,' he added quietly. 'And this isn't for sharing. With anyone,' he warned.

'All right,' she agreed.

'She was Eva's younger sister. The baby of the family, much loved. They both spoilt her, treated her as though she were fragile. She wasn't, but that was the impression she gave. Petite, pretty and vulnerable.' He gave a small, grim, smile. 'She needed constant reassurance, constant attention. And she didn't want children. Not that I knew that then.' He gave a little shake of his head. 'I'm getting ahead of myself. We were married in the local church, a white wedding, but not so many frills because it had been arranged hastily. It was what we both wanted. What she wanted. I switched to local flights so that we could be together. I already had my architectural exams, not that I'd done much practical work, but then a friend asked me to help finance him, set up a business... I have money,' he said, almost as an afterthought.

'Yes, Eva mentioned that.'

He nodded. 'I have business interests all round the world. Some inherited from my father, some by my own endeavours. I didn't do much of the actual drawing at the practice, just helped out when he needed it, but I thought it would make a secure base for the future, for any children that came along.

'It wasn't, exactly, as I had imagined marriage to be,' he confessed sadly. 'There were highs, of course there were, but she often seemed—dissatisfied. She wouldn't talk about it, or tell me what was wrong. She didn't like being at *home*. She liked to go out all the time, spend money. A lot of what happened can be laid at my door. I wasn't blameless, Kerith,' he said sombrely. 'I left her alone more than was wise, trying to build up the business. I didn't *think*, and I should have done. And then she found out she was pregnant. She was furious but I thought, in my naivety, that once the baby was born.... I can't even pretend it was postnatal depression. She wanted attention, Kerith. Wanted to be loved, which is natural, but she seemed to need constantly telling that she was pretty, admired. I wasn't as patient as I could have been, and maybe the faults were mine, but I did try. Thought I was doing all the right things. Went to baby classes...' His mind obviously back in the past, he sighed. 'I was there at the birth, and I loved that little baby, and I thought that she wouldn't be able to help but love him too. Which I think she did, but—it was like play acting. A little girl with a doll...' He sighed again as though it was still painful. 'She wanted a nanny,' he continued, 'or an au pair, which I found hard to understand, but when she had them, they weren't right either. She'd been spoilt all her life, had never worked, been independent, had everything done for her and so she found it hard to cope I think, run a house, look after a baby.'

'Childish?' she asked carefully.

'Yes.'

Reading a great deal into what he wasn't saying, she took his hand. 'Go on.'

'She became petulant, started going out a lot, and I thought it would do her good. Get it out of her system. To tell the truth, I was a bit bewildered by it all and yes, angry. My parents hadn't been like that. My friends' wives weren't like that. I did try, Kerith, but maybe not hard enough. I thought it would all get better. And then, when Michael was a few months old, I came home early one day. It was the nanny's day off.'

She squeezed his hand.

'She was in bed, our bed, with another man. Michael was in his cot in the corner.' He looked at Kerith, searched her face. 'Apparently it wasn't the first lover she'd had since we were married.'

'And so you took Michael and left.'

'Yes. I did go back to see her when I'd calmed down. She thought I would forgive her.'

'And you couldn't?'

'No. She didn't believe it at first, that I wouldn't go back to her. Couldn't seem to understand what the fuss was all about, as though everything that had happened was—normal.'

'And you never told Lena or Eva the truth?'

'I didn't need to. They knew the truth.'

Shocked, she just stared at him. 'They *knew*?'

'Yes. *Everyone* knew. That was what was so hard to take. Everyone knew but me. And I should have known, shouldn't I? Too busy with my own concerns, trying to build up the business, and none of it would have mattered, Kerith. I could have afforded to spend more time at home. I didn't even *need* to work.'

'Yes, you did,' she said gently. 'Men do need to work. But, if Eva knew the truth, why does she hate you so?'

'Because anything else would be a betrayal of her sister,' he said simply. 'She loved her, adored her, was very protective of her. She'd told me that Ginny wasn't ready for marriage. I arrogantly disregarded her fears. She thinks that, if Ginny hadn't married me, she wouldn't have died. And maybe she wouldn't.'

'But if she hadn't married you, there is every possibility she would have married someone else,' she pointed out.

'Yes, but that someone might have been more—available. I don't know, Kerith. Lena always said that Ginny was a tragedy waiting to happen, and maybe she was, but I contributed to her problems. If I hadn't been away so much, if I'd sought Lena or Eva's help...'

'That's hindsight, Tris.'

'Yes, but it doesn't take away the blame. I understand Eva's anger, and I wish it were different, that we could be friends.'

'But she won't forgive you, or herself,' she said softly.

'No, and I can't blame her for that. What I *can* blame her for is saying that I don't look after Michael, because she *knows* that isn't true. But when she's angry, she lashes out with everything she has. She's very—intransigent—where her sister's concerned. She always maintained that Ginny's affairs were a cry for help. Because I didn't love her as much as I should have done. Perhaps they were. And she owed it to her sister's memory to warn you off, because she likes you and didn't want to see you hurt. She knew I'd stayed in your apartment because Michael told her so when we went to Greece.'

'And so she anguished about it?' she said guessing. 'Imagined all sorts of things? And then, when she saw us together...' It had all come spilling out. All the anger, the feeling of history repeating itself? Not that Eva cared for her as she had her sister, but she was *fond* of her. Looking up at him, at his sombre face, she asked quietly, 'You didn't walk out on your partner, did you?'

'No. When I took Michael and left, I went to him. He'd known what was going on, as had all my friends, apparently, but no one knew how to tell me. I stayed with him and his wife for a few days and then took Michael down to my mother. I went back to flying, stayed with Michael and my mother in between trips. I continued to finance my partner, persuaded him to take on someone else and then, when my mother died, a few years later, I took Michael with me on my travels. I bought this house, the rest you know.'

No, she didn't. 'Suzanne?' she asked to give herself time.

He gave a small smile. 'I'd employed her to look after the house, keep an eye on Michael whilst I was working. She was useless, so I sacked her. Eva happened to ring one day to change some arrangements for seeing Michael and Suzanne answered. Her English wasn't very good, and Eva got hold of the wrong end of the stick. I didn't see her again for quite a while.'

'And so, not only does Eva blame you,' she said guessing slowly, 'but also herself for not fighting harder to get you both back together?'

He watched her and said nothing.

'She didn't want to bring the baby up? Or Lena?'

'Lena thought he would be better off with me. And told Eva so.'

'But, for Michael's sake, you couldn't cut all ties, could you?'

'No, although we manage to avoid each other pretty well,' he said sadly.

'Which was why you'd arranged to meet at a railway station in France and not at your house.'

'Yes.'

'And you don't blame Eva, do you?'

'No.'

And that was all he was going to say on the subject, because it wasn't his way to talk about people behind their backs. And she loved him for that.

Scrambling to her knees, she put her arms round him, rested her head on his shoulder. 'How long after you left did Ginny die?' she asked softly.

'Six months. I'd just started divorce proceedings. I'd already given her the house, which she sold. I didn't pay her maintenance, that was true, but she did have money in her account that I'd put there when we married. But I refused to listen to stories about her wildness after we'd split up. Refused to see her after that first time. And so she died.'

Horrified, she just stared at him. 'It wasn't your fault!'

'Wasn't it?'

'No!'

'But maybe I contributed to it by my behaviour. It will always be on my conscience.'

'Oh, Tris!' she exclaimed helplessly.

'And on Eva's,' he added quietly. 'But I find it hard to be *kind* to her.'

Because things had been said that couldn't be unsaid? But he could mend her plugs, fly out to Greece to make sure she was all right. He might say it was for Michael's sake, but she didn't think that was entirely true. He felt guilty for the broken marriage, blamed himself for Ginny's death, and yet none of it had been his fault. If we could see into the future, we could *all* be perfect, she thought. There would be no need of hindsight.

Piecing it all together from the things Eva had said, she queried softly, 'Ginny started going out with a lot of different men? Had a lot of exotic holidays with the money from the sale of the house? Was she trying to make you jealous? Go back to her?'

He didn't answer, but then, she hadn't expected he would.

'And then she died,' she added sadly.

'Yes, skiing off-piste in Switzerland. She hit a tree. I identified the body.'

'But no one said it was suicide, did they?'

'No.'

'Do *you* think it was?'

He sighed. 'No, I don't think it was deliberate. I think she was showing off. She was a spoilt child, Kerith, but she didn't deserve to die.'

'And so you tread a fine line between Lena and Eva,' she said gently.

He looked at her with a sort of bewilderment. 'You believe in me utterly, don't you?'

'Yes. You've never told anyone before, have you? Never excused, or reasoned.'

'No. Not even my mother.' He gave a small smile. 'She believed in me too. You would have got on well together I think.'

'And Lena does have room for you, doesn't she?'

'Yes. That was a lie, but for Eva's sake, Lena and I maintain the fiction to Michael that the bed would be too short, that I like my own space. And if he knows more than he's saying, then he keeps very quiet about it. He protects me. So fierce,' he added softly.

'Because you're *his*. Because he loves you. You said, you and Lena… Does that mean *she* doesn't blame you?'

'No, she's another one who blames herself because she gave in to Ginny's pleas to be married knowing what a disaster it would be.' He gave a small smile. 'You'd like her. She thinks she let me down, ruined my life. She knew the marriage would be wrong for both of us. Knew I would get hurt, because she knew, better than anyone, what Ginny was like. But because of Eva's—anger, because Eva is her daughter and she loves her, we pretend that we don't get on. Michael goes to stay with Lena in the holidays and sees Eva whenever *he* wants. Which has been really rather frequent since he met you.'

Startled, she just looked at him.

He smiled again. 'You didn't know? He never used to stay with Eva until you moved in across the way. He saw you, he liked you and said he would stay with Eva Friday nights instead of her babysitting at Lena's.'

'And Eva knew?'

'I imagine she could put two and two together,' he said drily.

'But she didn't seem to *mind* me having him.'

'No, because her social life came first, and because she didn't expect us to ever meet, but if we *did*, well, I was like your father and the last person you would ever—want. It's not a pretty story, Kerith.'

'No.'

'And you will never, ever, tell him what I have just told you.'

'No,' she agreed gently.

'Not in temper, not in...'

She touched his face. 'No. You can trust me.'

'I pray so. I can't have him hurt, Kerith. I can't.'

'Which is why you were so reluctant to marry again. In case it all happened again.' Was *still* a little afraid, she thought, and a part of him regretted having to tell her at all. She knew that. 'Eva won't tell him?' she asked worriedly. 'If she could spout off to me like that, isn't there a danger she'll tell Michael?'

'No,' he said definitely. 'She loves him, and she wouldn't deliberately do anything to hurt him. In her heart of hearts she *knows* how much I love him, but she can't forgive me, and I can't blame her for that.'

'No,' she agreed. 'But I'm not like Ginny,' she added slowly, carefully. 'And although I've never had a proper relationship before, I don't need waiting on hand, foot and finger. And knowing what happened before, well, we'll both be extra careful, won't we? And I will *tell* you if something is troubling me.'

He nodded.

'No more questions,' she promised. 'It won't be mentioned again.' And she wouldn't let him down. Whatever happened, she would never tell.

'When he was old enough to ask,' he continued, 'I simply told Michael that his mother and I had fallen out of love, that it happened, and that she had loved him. I didn't tell him she never saw him after we left.' Turning her so that he could see her face, he said quietly, 'I couldn't bear to have to tell him again. Still want to marry me?'

'Yes.'

'Because you believe me?'

'Yes,' she agreed simply. And she did. Wholeheartedly.

He closed his eyes and rested his head on top of hers. 'I'm a family man at heart, Kerith. It's what I've always wanted. I don't like living alone. I want someone to share with. To hear the sound of children's laughter. To be loved. Will you be able to live here? I wouldn't like to disrupt Michael's schooling, but…'

'Of course I can live here. I shall learn French. *Le bid is wid you, M'sieu,*' she mimicked, and he laughed, as she had meant him to.

'Can we have children?'

'God willing.'

He searched her beautiful face, her eyes, gently touched his fingers to her cheek. 'What about your new job?'

She gave a wry smile. 'From something that mattered so much, the be all and end all of my existence, it now doesn't matter at all,' she explained simply. 'Only you matter. You fill my heart and my mind to the exclusion of all else.'

'Dear God,' he whispered as his fingers tightened against her face. 'I don't believe this is happening.'

And he was afraid it wasn't real. 'It's real,' she affirmed as she took his hand and squeezed it. 'Miss Bossy has turned to putty.'

He lifted her hand to his mouth. 'How long can you stay?'

'To the end of the week. I have to go back, Tris, it's unfair not to.'

'I know.'

'I have to give a month's notice.'

'Which will take us to the beginning of November—and there's the school bus,' he added all in the same breath.

'Then, I'll see you tonight. Alone, and we can make love,' she said huskily and with a definite dip in her stomach.

His eyes darkened and he hugged her to him impossibly tight and kissed her as though he would never stop. He got abruptly to his feet, held out his hand to her, and then asked, 'Can we tell him?'

She nodded, gave him a shaky smile.

'Sure? He'll tell Eva.'

'I know. I'll handle it.' And she promised herself that she would never give him cause to be hurt like that again.

'Thank you.'

They walked hand in hand downstairs just as Michael erupted through the front door. Hair untidy, tie askew, satchel trailing in one hand, he halted, then grinned. 'Kerith!' He sounded absolutely delighted to see her. 'Why did no one tell me you were coming?'

'No one knew.' She smiled.

'We're going to be married,' Tris told him gently.

His eyes widened, his grin widened, and he threw his satchel in the air. 'Yes!'

She laughed. Well, that was a positive enough reaction.

'Didn't I tell you?' he asked his father. 'Didn't I *tell* you she was the one? Does Claude know?'

He shook his head.

Turning, he grabbed the knob on the front door, and then he halted. 'Hey. If you're going to be married...' Slowly turning back to face them, he asked seriously, 'Can I have a sister?'

Lips twitching, Tris promised, 'We'll do our best.'

'Neat. Jean Luc's got a sister and she loves him to bits. I'd like that.'

'You're already loved to bits,' Tris pointed out.

'Yes, I know,' he agreed confidently, 'but a sister, well, that's sort of special, isn't it? A *baby*!'

Feeling a lump form in her throat, Kerith hastily swallowed and squeezed Tris's hand tight.

Michael wrenched open the front door and could be heard calling urgently for Claude.

'Well, that was easy,' she said thickly.

He glanced at her. 'Crying, Kerith?' he asked softly and with a suspicious huskiness of his own.

'Just a bit,' she confessed. 'He made it sound—special.'

'It is special.'

CHAPTER EIGHT

'Are you all right?' Michael asked quietly.

She opened her eyes. 'I'm fine.' She smiled.

'Do you need anything?'

She shook her head.

'All right, I'll just be out front if you need me. Alexandra's still asleep.'

'Good. And Michael?' she called as he tiptoed away, 'Thank you.'

He came back and looked at her with a quizzical expression. 'What for?'

'Oh, for being you,' she said simply. 'For being the best son anyone could wish to have.'

He blushed, looked awkward for a moment, then dropped a hasty, and rather embarrassed, kiss on her cheek. 'I love you.'

'I know,' she agreed gently. 'As I love you.'

'We're so happy Kerith, aren't we?'

'Yes,' she agreed. 'We are.'

She watched him leave, and closed her eyes again. Yes, they were happy. Unbelievably so.

'Are you all right?' Tris asked.

She opened her eyes. 'I'm fine.'

'Don't need anything? Tea, coffee, something to eat?'

'No, thank you.'

'Warm enough?'

'Yes.'

'Baby's still asleep.'

'Mmm.' Staring up at this husband of hers, she gave a soft laugh. 'I've never known two such fusspots. I'm fine, really.'

'You still look very pale. Wouldn't you be better off by the fire?'

'No,' she said firmly.

'You mustn't get cold,' he warned as he tucked the blanket more warmly round her.

'I'm *not* cold! Go away. No, stay.' Holding out her hand to him, she smiled as he took it gently between his palms.

'I'm not made of glass.'

'You had a tough time.'

'I had a *baby*!'

He crouched down beside her and held her hand to his mouth. His beautiful eyes serious, solemn, he said, 'You frightened me to death.'

'I know,' she agreed gently. 'It probably won't be that bad next time.'

He shook his head. 'Oh, no, I can't go through that again.'

'We'll see,' she said comfortingly.

'You should have stayed in the hospital a few more days...'

'I wanted to come home.'

Home. How lovely that sounded. The house was full of flowers, full of gifts, from *everyone*! Each day Tris, or Michael, or both, would bring her something, some little present. A late-blooming flower, an interesting stone, a cake from the patisserie. She was so lucky. So very lucky.

Staring past him, through the glass doors, at the open fields, the beginnings of her garden, she saw that the late-flowering jasmine was coming into bloom. Amused at herself because, until recently, she had known absolutely *nothing* about gardens, she turned her eyes back to Tris. 'I wanted to come home,' she repeated.

'And we wanted you home. The house was very cold without you. I love you.'

'I know. Go on, go and finish your drawing. They want it by tomorrow.'

He gave a small grimace and got to his feet. 'Call if you need anything.'

'I will.'

He bent to kiss her and then returned to his drawing-board—which he'd set up at the opposite end of the spacious lounge so that he could keep an eye on her.

Cosseted, pampered, loved. Who could ask for more? She couldn't believe how contented she'd been. She didn't miss working at all. She maybe would when Alexandra was older.

The year had gone so fast. They'd been married

here in the little church in November, with the whole village in attendance. Her friends had come, and her mother. Who had cried. That had surprised her. She'd also been surprised to receive a letter from Lena. A nice letter, a kind letter, wishing her happiness and saying how sorry she was not to be able to come to the wedding. Because it would have hurt Eva.

And now it was November again, and her mother would be coming out in a few days to see her granddaughter. She wished that Lena could come too. And Eva. She hoped that one day Eva would forgive herself and others.

Turning her head, Kerith glanced at the carry-cot. A daughter. It seemed so unbelievable. Everyone in the village had been so kind, even going so far as to learn some English so that they could communicate with her. But then, they would do anything for Tris, she had discovered. That had surprised her— no, not surprised, delighted and pleased her, and she couldn't imagine, now, why she had ever believed him lightweight. He wasn't. He was caring and thoughtful, responsible. Still a little afraid, she thought, to believe in this happiness, but such a special man.

And she loved him. More and more, each day. And if she'd believed Eva... No, she wouldn't think of that. But she did feel sorry for the other girl. Both

Eva and Ginny searching for something neither of them had been able to find.

She heard a burst of laughter from the garden, and smiled. Michael and his friend, Jean Luc. She was so proud of him, this young stepson of hers, and she thoroughly envied his ability to switch from French to English to French. One day, she promised herself, and she would be as fluent as he.

There had been no jealousy that she now shared his father. And certainly no jealousy over the baby. It was *his* baby.

And, as if she knew she was being thought about, Alexandra stirred, gave a little cry. She would want feeding. Not that Kerith would have to get up; in seconds both Tris and Michael would be there to help. They wanted her awake, to see her eyes open, her hands flutter. Anyone would think she was the only baby in the world. The most perfect, the most special, the cleverest baby in the whole world. As she was, of course.

'She's awake,' Tris said softly just as Michael tiptoed in.

'Is she awake?' Michael asked, saw his father, and grinned. He walked over to the cot, and leaned in. 'Hello, sweetheart?' he said softly. 'Are you getting hungry?' He wiped his fingers on his jeans and then put one into her hand and smiled as she automatically grasped it. 'I think she's smiling,' he said hopefully.

'I expect she is,' Kerith agreed. 'What little girl wouldn't want to smile at such a nice big brother?'

His smile was just that little bit proud. 'Jean Luc said he would like to see her. Can he?'

'Yes, of course.'

He retreated to the door and beckoned. Fair-haired, grubby, a little taller than Michael, Jean Luc smiled at her. *'Bonjour, madame,'* he greeted politely.

'Bonjour, Jean Luc. Comment allez-vous?'

He grinned. *'Très bien, madame, et vous?'*

'Très bien,' she agreed with a wide smile of her own.

'Bon.' He glanced towards the carry-cot. *'Bébé?'*

'Oui.'

They all spoke in simple phrases, and very slowly, so that she would understand.

Michael came to draw the curtain across the window—just in *case* there was a draught, and Tris lifted his daughter from the cot, cuddled her against him for a moment, stared down into her perfect face, and smiled with so much love and contentment that Kerith felt almost overwhelmed.

He showed his precious burden to Michael's friend, even allowed him to touch a finger to her nose, which surprised her because the finger was absolutely filthy, and then carried her across to Kerith.

She could feel a laugh bubbling up inside her for

the expression on Jean Luc's face. He looked utterly astonished at this ritual. As well he might. She winked at him and he giggled.

Tris said something to him in French that Kerith *thought* meant, 'You must think us very strange' and he laughed even harder.

'We aren't strange!' Michael protested.

'No,' Tris agreed with a warm smile for his son, 'just adoring.'

'Yes,' Michael agreed. 'We are, aren't we? But I'll be glad when she can sit up and talk.' Switching to French, he said something to his friend, and they both went out.

A smile in his eyes, Tris murmured ruefully, 'That will be all round the village tomorrow.'

'As if you care.'

'Mmm,' he agreed softly. 'As if I care.' He gently touched the baby's dark hair. 'They all think me mad anyway.'

'In love,' she corrected.

'Yes. In love. So very much in love.'

Modern Romance™
...seduction and passion guaranteed

Tender Romance™
...love affairs that last a lifetime

Sensual Romance™
...sassy, sexy and seductive

Blaze
...sultry days and steamy nights

Medical Romance™
...medical drama on the pulse

Historical Romance™
...rich, vivid and passionate

29 new titles every month.

With all kinds of Romance for every kind of mood...

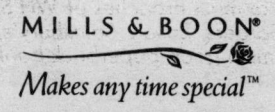

MILLS & BOON®
Makes any time special™

MAT4

MILLS & BOON

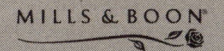

Tender Romance™

EMMA'S WEDDING by Betty Neels

Meeting Dr Roele van Dyke was a blessing for Emma: he went out of his way to make her happy. When Roele had to return to Amsterdam permanently, he couldn't leave Emma behind – so he offered her a job. But did he want her to be his secretary – or his wife?

PART-TIME MARRIAGE by Jessica Steele

Elexa was determined to stop her family bugging her about finding a man to marry. Wealthy businessman Noah Peverelle offered a solution: he wanted a son, but not a wife... A convenient, part-time marriage seemed ideal – only it turned out to be not so temporary!

MORE THAN A MILLIONAIRE by Sophie Weston

Emilio Diz was an irresistible millionaire and he wanted a woman to perfect his image – a trophy wife! Abby – Lady Abigail Templeton-Burke – needed Emilio's help and was ideal for creating the right impression. But Abby was driving him crazy – with desire!

BRIDE ON THE LOOSE by Renee Roszel

Jumping off a yacht in the dead of night was the most irresponsible thing Dana had ever done – but she'd been forced to escape her double-crossing fiancé! Luckily, she was rescued by a gorgeous stranger, Sam. Now she faced another complication: she was falling for Sam – fast!

On sale 2nd November 2001

Available at most branches of WH Smith, Tesco, Martins, Borders, Eason, Sainsbury's, Woolworths and most good paperback bookshops.

1101/59/MB22

MILLS & BOON

Christmas
with a Latin Lover

Three brand-new stories

Lynne Graham
Penny Jordan
Lucy Gordon

Published 19th October

Available at most branches of WH Smith, Tesco, Martins, Borders, Eason, Sainsbury's, Woolworths and most good paperback bookshops.

The perfect gift this Christmas from

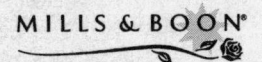

MILLS & BOON®

3 brand new romance novels and a FREE French manicure set

for just £7.99

featuring best selling authors
Betty Neels,
Kim Lawrence and Nicola Cornick

Available from 19th October

Available at most branches of WH Smith, Tesco, Martins, Borders, Eason, Sainsbury's, Woolworths and most good paperback bookshops.

1101/94/MB28

MILLS & BOON
FOREIGN AFFAIRS
A captivating 12 book collection of sun-kissed seductions.
Enjoy romance around the world
DON'T MISS BOOK 1
greek grooms–
Passion in the Mediterranean sun
Amazing value 2-in-1 title
Introductory price
£2.99
Available from 5th October
Available at most branches of WH Smith, Tesco, Martins, Borders, Eason, Sainsbury's, Woolworths and most good paperback bookshops.
FA/RTL/1

Helen Bianchin Margaret Way Jessica Hart

3 Full-length novels ONLY **£4.99** IR £6.45

MILLS & BOON®

Weddings Down Under

Australian men...to the altar!

Available 2nd November

Available at most branches of WH Smith, Tesco, Martins, Borders, Eason, Sainsbury's, Woolworths and most good paperback bookshops.

2 FREE
books and a surprise gift!

We would like to take this opportunity to thank you for reading this Mills & Boon® book by offering you the chance to take TWO more specially selected titles from the Tender Romance™ series absolutely FREE! We're also making this offer to introduce you to the benefits of the Reader Service™—

- ★ FREE home delivery
- ★ FREE gifts and competitions
- ★ FREE monthly Newsletter
- ★ Exclusive Reader Service discounts
- ★ Books available before they're in the shops

Accepting these FREE books and gift places you under no obligation to buy, you may cancel at any time, even after receiving your free shipment. Simply complete your details below and return the entire page to the address below. *You don't even need a stamp!*

YES! Please send me 2 free Tender Romance books and a surprise gift. I understand that unless you hear from me, I will receive 4 superb new titles every month for just £2.49 each, postage and packing free. I am under no obligation to purchase any books and may cancel my subscription at any time. The free books and gift will be mine to keep in any case.

N1ZEA

Ms/Mrs/Miss/Mr ....Initials................................
BLOCK CAPITALS PLEASE

Surname ....

Address ....

....

....Postcode................................

Send this whole page to:
UK: FREEPOST CN81, Croydon, CR9 3WZ
EIRE: PO Box 4546, Kilcock, County Kildare (stamp required)

Offer valid in UK and Eire only and not available to current Reader Service subscribers to this series. We reserve the right to refuse an application and applicants must be aged 18 years or over. Only one application per household. Terms and prices subject to change without notice. Offer expires 30th April 2002. As a result of this application, you may receive offers from other carefully selected companies. If you would prefer not to share in this opportunity please write to The Data Manager at the address above.

Mills & Boon® is a registered trademark owned by Harlequin Mills & Boon Limited.
Tender Romance™ is being used as a trademark.